Forbidden Desires

Irish Honor, Volume 3

Amara Holt

Published by Amara Holt, 2024.

Prologue

Tulia

Past

One street and another. I don't even know where I'm going. The scenery blurs, confusing my already exhausted mind.

Running was never a necessity, so today, when I need to do it, it feels like my heart is going to burst out of my chest. Despite that, I don't stop; even on a horrible day, in the middle of a Kentucky winter, I run, and I run because I need to escape.

Maybe if I keep running, the scene I just witnessed will fade from my memory?

A kilometer? Two? I couldn't say.

I run out of cowardice, out of fear of facing what happened, but no matter how hard I try, it's useless. I will never forget what I saw.

The cold air makes my lungs feel like they're about to explode, but I don't care about the pain the freezing weather causes my body. It doesn't even come close to the pain inside my heart.

I've left everything behind: keys, documents, my dreams.

Especially them, there is nothing left.

I don't allow myself to cry yet. I just keep running, even without knowing where I'm going.

No more family Christmases; no more plans for a happy future.

I feel like all my nerves are twitching inside my body, in sync with the way my feet hit the ground.

I was never afraid. I was born into the Russian mafia.

Father, cousins of both sexes, all my relatives owe their allegiance to the Pakhan.

I am not a princess; I am a proletarian. A girl whose family and fiancé are mere soldiers of the Organization.

Despite not being among the elite, discipline and obedience have always been part of the routine.

Conformity, too.

I am my mother's mirror in every way.

But now, I will need to reinvent myself.

The Tulia who let others tell her what to do is gone. The girl who believed that being a good girl would make her happy, because life owed her that, is gone too.

At the moment, I am an empty shell.

A void. A nothing.

The bad side is that I am heartbroken and lost.

The good side is that I am heartbroken and lost.

My weakness is also my strength.

My lack of direction, my compass.

Chapter 1

Tulia

Two Years Later

*N*o, *this is not right!*
   Damn it! Is it so hard to put things in the right order?
   I look at a row of books in the public library, irritated by the carelessness of whoever was responsible for this *mistake,* unacceptable to my eyes.
   In fact, I'm sure it's unacceptable to anyone with OCD.
   "*Why won't you come?*" my sister asks on the phone, bringing me back to reality, even though I'm still staring at the disorganized books. "*I understand that something serious must have happened between you and Simeon for you to leave everything behind, but do you think it's fair to take it out on the family, Tulia? It's our parents' wedding anniversary.*"
   I wipe my forehead, which is now covered in a layer of cold sweat. I need to take a deep breath before I respond because just the thought of meeting my relatives again makes me feel nauseous.
   "I'm not ready to see the family yet."
   I'll never be ready to see them again.
   "*Look, I'm going to give you some advice. I know that in the Organization there are therapists who deal with women with problems like yours. My neighbor is the wife of a soldier of the Brotherhood like our father and managed to get an appointment after an attempted rape,*"

she says. "*She even told me that now she almost never thinks about the incident anymore.*"

As if it were that simple to resolve!

You flip a switch in your mind, or in this case, go to a session, and all the trauma vanishes into thin air.

It's a pity for her theory that dealing with feelings and emotions is much more complex.

"Are you advising me to see one? Why are you so sure the problem is with me, Alla? Why couldn't it be with Simeon?"

When she remains silent for what feels like seconds but seems like hours, I finally understand.

They always considered my ex-fiancé too good for me.

More *handsome,* more *intelligent,* more *charming.*

I even heard from my mother that I should be grateful he chose me.

"*Yes, I think maybe you should seek help since you don't want to tell any of us what happened,*" she finally says.

"I'm fine, Alla. Go live your life with your children and husband."

She hesitates for a moment.

"*I'm not completely happy either, you know? We have to adapt.*"

I sigh, feeling irritation flood every cell of my body.

"That's what Mom taught us, right? To adapt, I mean." I let out a humorless laugh. "Here's the bad news, sister: I tried. I did everything I was told my whole life, and guess what? It didn't help at all."

"*What do you mean by that?*"

"Forget it. Some things are better left in the past. Trust me."

"*Look, any mistake you made...*"

"Mistake that *I* made?"

"*The way you said it, it sounds like you betrayed him.*"

Oh God, I need to hang up or I'll end up doing something I'll regret forever.

"I have to go."

"*When will we talk again?*"

"Send a message. When I can, I'll reply. Take care."

I hang up the phone and press my forehead against the bookshelf, trying to calm down.

Who needs therapy? I don't. What I need is to be cleared for my first mission to finally unload my anger on someone—and if it's on an enemy of the Organization, I won't feel any remorse.

"Did you find what you were looking for, my dear?" The elderly librarian approaches me.

"Actually, no, but I noticed these books are out of place," I reply, gesturing towards the aisle where we are.

She furrows her brow.

"They are?"

"Yes. The series are in the wrong order. If you notice, this one, for example, jumps from book five to eight, then comes two..." *And it's driving me crazy,* I think but don't say. Instead, I force a fake smile and continue: "It would be easier for anyone looking if they were in order."

She adjusts her glasses and checks. Then she looks at me as if I've discovered the cure for cancer.

"You're right, they are. Unfortunately, I'll need to wait for some internal assistants. It could take up to a week for a request like this to be addressed."

I could turn my back and leave because this isn't my problem, but I know I won't be able to sleep at night if I do. I'll be tossing and turning in bed, imagining those books out of order.

I'm aware that I developed compulsions after what happened two years ago. Some people turn to vices: alcohol, food.

I developed a compulsion for physical exercise and extreme organization.

How did I figure this out? After rearranging my clothes in the dresser more than ten times in one week, I realized something was wrong and looked it up online. Not that understanding this has helped reduce the compulsion, but at least I know there's a name for what I have: obsessive-compulsive disorder.

"I could check everything and fix it for you," I offer.

She looks around as if searching for an ambulance to take me to the asylum.

"My dear, no offense, but did you notice the size of this room?"

"I don't see any problem. It'll count as a good deed, and maybe God will forgive me a sin or two for helping you."

"I'd feel bad, as if I were exploiting you."

"Believe me, you won't be."

I was informed that I would receive a mission soon, and I'm getting anxious with the wait. At least I'll make the time pass.

Four hours later, I start to consider taking my sister's advice and seeing a psychologist after all. "Talking about the past might be a way to avoid numbing my brain with physical effort and at least save my spine," I think with irony.

Every muscle in my body aches, and I feel like I've had a severe beating.

I get home, strip off my clothes as quickly as I can, and, still in my underwear and bra, get into the shower, moaning loudly as the hot water starts working its miracle on my exhausted body.

I wrap myself in a towel and am ready to eat and sleep, when suddenly, I see there's a message on my phone.

My heart races as I confirm it's from Fanya, my cousin, who I actually consider a sister now, also a soldier of the Russian Organization and the reason I joined the Brotherhood.

I read and reread the message more than once, unable to believe it.

Finally, after two years, I'm going to start living.

Chapter 2

Tulia

Somewhere in Arizona — United States

I check myself in the mirror one last time before leaving the roadside motel room where I've been staying.

Yes, I think I pass as a typical small-town girl — frayed denim shorts and a plaid shirt.

Not that the appearance is far from my "real" self; the only difference between how I dress now and how I dressed in my hometown is that with the top two buttons undone, I reveal much more skin and the curve between my breasts than I normally would.

I look at the handmade red leather boots. They're not part of the costume; they're actually mine, and I love them.

As soon as I started earning some money within the Organization, I got rid of almost all my belongings, but I couldn't bring myself to throw these away.

They are what's left of my old life: a pair of boots and a broken heart.

I shake my head, forcing myself to stop this path of self-pity.

Two years have passed, and despite becoming, like my cousin, a soldier, a member of the Organization, receiving military-grade training, and learning to fight and defend myself physically, inside, I sometimes still feel like a girl.

Enough, Tulia. Focus on tonight. Remember the instructions you received.

I grab the document with the fake surname and some money, tucking them into the back pocket of my shorts.

Then, I pull out my phone and check the name of my mission.

Sierra — the woman who is the daughter of the most powerful enemy of the Brotherhood right now: Fernando Morales, the head of the Mexican drug cartel *Los Morales*.

"I'm ready," I say to myself half an hour later as I follow her car down the highway.

I know she drives around every night, and at first, I thought she'd stop somewhere, but no. She just drives randomly. It's ironic that we share the same habit.

I still don't understand what the daughter of a cartel boss is doing alone in the middle of Arizona, but Fanya explained from the start that in our line of work, the less you snoop, the better.

"Do your job and don't look around," *my cousin said.* "Never try to find out more than what you've been given in the mission. And, most importantly, never form a bond with your target."

I think about the woman who is now the closest relative I have.

The funny thing is, we never got along. Fanya is unyielding, prickly, and despite loving her with all my heart, she can be a cruel witch most of the time.

And yet, she was the one who saved me when I needed a helping hand. The only one I had the courage to tell what I saw and, most importantly: who stood up to the family on my behalf, explaining that I would not be coming home anymore.

After everything, during this time away, I've only spoken to my sister on the phone a few times.

With Simeon, I ended up returning the zirconia ring — yes, the bastard didn't even have the decency to give me a real jewel — by mail.

We never talked about the incident. He tried to contact me once, but my cousin told him that if he persisted, she would report everything to the Pakhan, so he backed off, believing I would stay silent as well. Soon, I realized Fanya was right from the start when she advised me to join the Brotherhood. Only in this way would I be protected from both traitors.

I shake my head as if that could clear away the memories and force myself to stay focused on tonight, but I frown when I see Sierra pulling into the parking lot of a restaurant with a huge glowing sign advertising a beer brand.

She parks the car and after she turns off the headlights, I do the same, parking a row behind.

It's deserted, so there's a small risk she might see me, but the instructions were to make first contact with her tonight, and I can't postpone.

What are you doing standing there, you idiot? Either go into the damn restaurant or leave so I can proceed with my plan — *which basically involves pretending that my car broke down in the parking lot of the motel where she's staying.*

It would be a much better approach than inside a bar. Women always feel sympathetic towards others in need. When they're out hunting for fun, which seems to be what Sierra came for, they are more skittish and territorial.

If Morales' daughter had been a good girl and done the usual — driving around aimlessly before finally returning to her lonely motel room — I would pretend to be an innocent guest who knows nothing about cars, needing help.

Both a round lie — I left my innocence behind two years ago and love tinkering with car engines. My grandfather was a mechanic.

Instead of sticking to my original plan, however, I'm about to enter a bar with the daughter of one of Mexico's biggest drug traffickers because, no matter what, I need to introduce myself into Sierra's life tonight. There's no way I'm going to break orders right off the bat, on my first mission.

To make matters worse, I'm dressed as if I want to take someone to my hotel room tonight — which couldn't be further from the truth.

The idea was to look country and innocent enough that she wouldn't see me as a threat.

I finally see Sierra get out of the car. I follow her, taking care not to slam the door, while scanning the surroundings. I don't like open spaces, especially at night, and I conclude that the woman must know how to defend herself or be suicidal because even for me, who received intense training, I don't think it's advisable to be wandering around a place like this alone.

She walks quickly and enters the bar, which at least shows she's not that stupid.

I let a few people pass in front of me, keeping a safe distance between me and Sierra. If I approach her now, she'll be suspicious.

Although I have no intention of drinking, I head to the bar and order a beer from the *bartender*, who has a grumpy expression.

The place is dark, and the music is annoying. Everyone seems either drunk or very willing to get that way.

The men look at me as if I'm a piece of meat, and instinctively, the coward in me checks my phone in the back pocket of my shorts. I could handle one or two of these idiots, but not all of them at once, unless I grab the gun I left in the car or the knife I carry in my boot.

"Can I buy you a drink, sweetheart?" The inevitable question comes less than five minutes later.

If I had made a bet with myself, I would have lost.

I could have sworn it would be the bearded blond guy in Wrangler jeans with a perfect ass who would come to me first. Instead, it's a kid who barely looks out of *High School.*

"They don't sell beer to anyone under twenty-one," I say, looking him up and down to make it clear he doesn't have a chance with me — besides, I already have mine.

He huffs.

"I made a bet with my friends, miss," he says, subtly nodding his head behind him. "If I don't get at least a smile from you, I'll have to lend my truck to each of them for the week. I can't be without my truck."

"Next time you make a deal, use your brain, not your ego."

His shoulders slump as if he's lost hope, and I'm not sure if I should give him a consoling hug or a punch for getting in the way of my mission.

I approach, wrapping my arms around his neck, and the kid starts to tremble.

"I'm going to give you a kiss right here," I whisper so only he can hear, pressing my lips to a patch of skin exposed by the collar of his shirt. "Smile and look like a sleaze. Then, I'll move away from you and have some fun. Don't follow me. I'm helping you out of pity. If you get in my way again, I'll rip off your balls and feed them to you."

Chapter 3

Tulia

I approached her gradually, coming across as if I were just a passerby, but even with all my caution, at first, she looked at me as if she wanted to kill me. That was the first thing I noticed: Sierra is incredibly suspicious.

"Wouldn't you be if you were the daughter of an international drug dealer?" *a voice whispers in my mind.*

I'm dying of curiosity to figure out this puzzle.

What on earth is a woman who could be protected by a cartel—and play the role of a drug lord's princess—doing lost in the middle of Arizona? Doesn't her father worry about the risks she's running? Because one thing is certain in this world: all criminal organizations, just like their families, are targets.

Maybe I'll never satisfy my curiosity, though, as orders within the Brotherhood are given to soldiers like me in dribs and drabs. Only the higher-ups know exactly what a mission entails. All I've been told is that I need to make her trust me and then offer her a "job."

Finally, I stop at the pool table where she's playing alone. Despite her beauty, none of the men have approached her. There's something about her that sends a clear message of "don't come near or I might kill you."

Sierra would be the type of person I'd like to have as a friend. It says a lot about a woman to have the courage to walk into a bar in the middle of nowhere and play alone without giving a damn about potential sexual predators.

She trusts herself, and her audacity is contagious in a male-dominated world.

Not many girls join organizations. Inside, we're respected because at least in the Russian one, it's a Pakhan's order that we're treated the same way as regular soldiers, but there's still prejudice and always a jerk or two making jokes or doubting our capabilities.

I'd be a liar if I didn't confess that, during the first few months of training, I thought about quitting, since I was raised to be a sweet housewife, but the anger inside me, along with the fear of what Simeon might do to me if I were alone and unprotected, kept me going.

I watch the woman, who seems about to make her next shot, but before she hits the cue ball, she looks up and meets my gaze.

She seems torn between ignoring me or talking to me, and if I were to bet, I'd say from her expression, the chance of her hurling a ball at my head is high, but seconds later, her face relaxes and I breathe again.

She gestures for me to come closer, and playing the part of the naive girl, I walk over hesitantly.

She looks at me as if I were from another planet, and I suspect it's because she thinks I shouldn't be in a bar full of men, alone.

Yeah, I kind of agree with you, Sierra, but since you changed your plans today, here we are.

I force myself to take action to avoid overplaying my role.

"Can I play?"

She shrugs.

"I'm already in the last round," she says.

"That's fine. I don't want to interrupt," I lie.

"If you were interrupting, I'd have kicked you out already."

"Alright. I'll stay then. Thanks."

"YOU SHOULDN'T COME to a bar like this alone, Tulia," she advises.

After playing two games of pool with Sierra, we sit down to chat.

With every word that comes out of her mouth, I feel worse for deceiving her, but I force myself to remember that she is the enemy's daughter and that if I don't complete my mission, dozens of Organization members could die at the hands of the Morales family.

That's what my rational side insists all the time, but my heart is definitely not as dead as I first thought, because I can feel Sierra's loneliness in her gaze, in the way she lets slip things about her journey, which, as far as I can tell, is not on the same path as her father's.

The plan is for me to lie to her, and I even have fake documents to back up this lie in case she investigates me. To Sierra, I am eighteen and not twenty-two, and as soon as she found out my *age*, she took the beer from my hand and replaced it with a soda.

She asked me a lot of questions, which was expected, and I lied, of course, saying that after reaching legal age, I left my parents' house.

I made up the rest too: that we were very poor and that I could hardly wait to set off into the world and live adventures.

If Sierra could see the Tulia from two years ago, she'd probably laugh at how pathetic I was. My biggest ambition was to have a house with a big backyard to raise my kids.

I push those thoughts away because whenever they come up, I get melancholic.

"I don't usually go out alone at night, but today I was feeling adventurous." And then, I take a deep breath because from now on, our conversation will be crucial. "I have a friend who promised to find me a job."

"A decent one?"

"Yes, indeed. I'll be fine, Ana," I reply, using the fake name she introduced herself with.

How could I judge her? I didn't give my real Russian last name, Pushkin, either, but a made-up one, London.

"But just in case," I continue, "could you give me your number? I don't want to seem like a baby or anything, but just in case something bad happens."

"No, I can't," she replies, and my heart sinks. *Jesus, I've failed!* "But I'll keep yours. I'll check in on you from time to time, just to see how things are going."

Chapter 4

Tulia

Weeks Later

❚❚ *Tulia?*" Sierra asks when she answers, and as has happened over the weeks since we met, the guilt hits me so hard that I want to vomit.

She told me she'd break her own rules, then she gave me her real name and phone number. All of this because she was worried about me—being alone in the United States.

Every time we hang up, I feel like crying.

I tried asking Fanya what they would do with her if I convince her to take the job in Wisconsin. My cousin said she didn't know, but they definitely wouldn't kill or sexually or physically assault her, because Pakhan's wife, Talassa, would never allow such things. Taking female prisoners is an exception, not the rule, according to my cousin, so I'm assuming she'll be kept as a hostage to have leverage against her father.

Knowing this doesn't ease my conscience.

God, if I'm already doubting so much on my first mission, how will I survive in this world for the rest of my life?

Feeling remorse doesn't suit the role of an Organization member, but it happens to me frequently.

Sierra checks in with me several times a week, and I feel more and more connected to her, but I know that if I decide to walk away now, it will mean betrayal to my superiors, and the punishment for that is death.

I'm not ready to die. I'm too young, but the doubts about whether this life is truly for me keep growing.

When I left home and went to stay with Fanya—who is despised by the entire family—I was lost. She not only gave me the option to live with her as a roommate, but she also offered to introduce me to the Brotherhood. Ultimately, she shielded me from the rest of the family—which was exactly what I wanted and needed at that moment.

Last week, I talked to her about my insecurity regarding continuing as an Organization soldier forever, and her response was that I could only leave if I married a member and became a housewife. Trying to leave on my own would be like signing my own death sentence.

Jesus, what should I do?

Every time she calls, Sierra advises me to be careful because, according to her, I'm the perfect prey for exploitative scoundrels. These details show me that, enemy's daughter or not, she has a good heart.

She's no longer in Arizona, and that was the only thing she hid from me: her current whereabouts.

"Sierra, I'm sorry to call you, but I'm kind of desperate," I say, finally resuming the conversation.

"Did something happen?"

"Um... Something good. I wanted to know if you could help me, though. That thing you mentioned the other day, about looking for a job as a housekeeper, a sort of family secretary, is it true?"

I know she has worked as a nanny during her travels around the country and that she occasionally takes a more or less permanent job. She never told me why she doesn't stay in one place, and this, combined with the fact that she doesn't seem to have much more money than I do, makes me think that perhaps my superiors are wrong and she doesn't want anything to do with her drug-dealing father.

"Yes, it is," she replies. "But I haven't found anything that fits what I need."

"You told me you prefer places further from the city. I don't... I love crowds. Anyway, I got a position that seems like a dream job because of the salary, but unfortunately, my father got sick, and I'll have to go back home for a couple of months."

I'm not sure I understand. Are you in need of money?

"Always, right? I'm poor, but in this particular case, it's not about that. I want to 'secure' this position. I'm afraid they'll put someone else in my place because they said they need someone immediately. I'll be honest with you: I can't give up this job because the salary is good, and I need the money, so what I'm offering you won't be permanent. As soon as things get better with my father, I'll want it back," I say, increasing the lies more and more.

I'm not looking for something long-term anyway.

"And I haven't even told you the best part: the employer, as far as I understand, is a reclusive man who spends some months a year in the Wisconsin mountains and others in his residence in Boston. Even that seems perfect. You'd be in an isolated place you love for the first few months, and when I return, I'll go to the big city."

She doesn't respond for several seconds, and I feel my heart pounding in my ears from nerves.

"*Send me his details by message,*" she says, and I'm torn between relief and the urge to say it was a mistake and there is no job, actually.

However, I know I can't backtrack now if I want to see the next sunrise.

"I don't even need to tell you that it's confidential, right? The guy is very wealthy, Sierra. I'm taking a leap of faith sharing this with you."

If he's so important, how will he accept a stranger in his place?

"I told him you were my best friend, which is not untrue since I don't trust any other woman but you," I reply, feeling worse and worse. "He'll want your details to check you out, of course."

"That's the least of my worries. I can provide it, but I want to verify him too."

"Why are you so suspicious?" I ask, still in the role I'm playing.

*"Why are you so naive?" she retorts, then continues: "*That was a rhetorical question, Tulia. People are what they are, a product of the environment they grew up in. Give me the name of this employer, and I'll check him out. I'll give you an answer later today."

She hangs up after saying goodbye, and I sit on the cheap motel bed, wanting to curl up in a corner and cry.

I know I need to stay in the Organization to keep protected *from them*, but I don't want to spend my life harming people like Sierra.

About three hours later, when she calls me to say everything is set and she'll take the job, I pack my bag and wait for orders from my superiors. As I expected, they don't take long to get in touch.

*"*Good job, Tulia. You should head to Boston now and await further instructions. For now, your mission is complete."

Chapter 5

Tulia

Boston

Months Later

I'm certain that if I stay locked in this apartment for one more day, I'll go insane.

Everything that could go wrong on my first mission did, in fact, go wrong. Starting with the fact that Sierra, my past target, is now Leonid's wife, which means I lured into a trap none other than the wife of one of Yerik's trusted men.

Of course, I was following orders, but who cares about such a trivial *detail*?

Not my superiors, certainly, as I have been living in something of a house arrest since their relationship was made official.

To make matters worse, Fanya, my cousin and the only person I had to talk to, made the stupid mistake of intervening out of jealousy of Leonid between Pakhan's underboss and Sierra.

Result: she only didn't die because I humbled myself, calling my former protector, now mortal enemy, Sierra, and begged for my cousin's life.

I'm increasingly convinced that she will never forgive me, which means my career in the Organization is over.

I recall the last time we spoke, a few months ago:

"Sierra, we need to talk."

I had been told that an order had been given for Fanya to be killed. I panicked and called Sierra, even though I knew I was the last person she wanted to hear from.

It wouldn't help to talk to Leonid. From everything I discovered, he was in love. He took any offense against his wife very seriously, and Fanya had crossed all the lines.

"You are very cynical to have the courage to call me, Tulia. By the way, is that really your name?"

"Yes, it is."

"Alright, then let me put it this way so you can understand: go fuck yourself, Tulia."

"I understand that you're angry."

"Angry? You sent me to my death, you bitch."

"Leonid won't kill you. You're his wife."

Yes, it wasn't a good argument, but it was all I had to work with at that moment. Only after the mission with Sierra was over did I realize how naive I had been. She was lucky to win the underboss's heart, because it became obvious to me, after thinking about her situation, that, regardless of whether Pakhan incurred Talassa's hatred, his wife, who doesn't tolerate violence against women, in that specific case, the plan should have been to kill her. And worse: Fanya knew and lied to me.

"You couldn't have been sure of that at the time and you didn't care what my fate would be. I risked myself for you. I was constantly fleeing from my father and his enemies and risked myself for you, worried about your safety, you bitch."

I remember she started to cry, and I, despite everything I had been through, never allowing myself to shed a tear, felt my cheeks wet as well.

Shame, guilt, pain, and loneliness, all mixed into an explosive package inside me.

"I'm so sorry, Sierra."

"Don't call me again. I thought we had ended this false friendship the last time we spoke."

"If it's any consolation, I spent days without sleeping thinking about you."

"It's no consolation, Tulia. If I weren't in a relationship with Leonid now; if the plans the Russians had for me had gone as expected, I'd be dead. I understand you were doing your job, but stay out of my way, damn it."

"I'm desperate," I said, because all I could think about was my cousin being killed.

"Whatever the reason, it's not my problem."

"Actually, it kind of is."

"I don't understand."

"Fanya is my sister. I mean, cousin-sister, but currently, she's closer to me than my biological sister."

"What? Well, now I'm not surprised that she's a bitch too."

"You can call me names all you want, but I beg you, don't let them kill her, Sierra. I don't have anyone else. I know what she did to you was awful—" *I continued, remembering the message I was given.*

Out of spite, my cousin told Sierra the truth about Leonid's initial plan to kill her, which made her flee and nearly get killed by one of the underboss's men, a traitor infiltrated in the Organization.

She should never have interfered in their relationship, but what in a normal situation would be punished by social exclusion, end of friendship, in the Brotherhood, the penalty for any kind of betrayal, whether by action or words, is death.

"What the hell are you talking about? Are you crazy?" she asked, and I was sure she didn't know how things would unfold from there.

"Go to the farm's barn. Talk to Leonid. Only you can make him change his mind. Please, I'm begging you."

"I..."

"Please, Sierra. Ask him to send her to Moscow. She'll hate it, but don't let them kill my sister."

It's only when I feel the desperation deep in my soul that I realize what Fanya has become: my sister, much more than the one born of the same mother that I could ever be.

Sierra hung up that night without giving me an answer, and I couldn't sleep. The next morning, however, I received a message from her saying that Fanya had been sent to Russia.

They never allowed us to speak, but I know she's alive because one of the soldiers stationed here in Boston had been to Moscow recently and spoke with her. Fanya's situation isn't much better than mine here. We're both prisoners, even if it's not explicitly stated. All I wonder is how much longer this situation will last.

Feeling crazy, I grab my helmet and motorcycle keys.

The order given to me is to never sleep away from home—yes, at almost twenty-three, I have a curfew.

But it's five o'clock. Enough time to at least breathe some fresh air away from this apartment.

I ride aimlessly for about half an hour, and when I realize the path I've taken, I shake my head.

Jesus, I'm really going crazy!

I've developed the strange habit of wandering through cemeteries. I walk among the gravestones, and strangely, I find peace in looking at the inscriptions and imagining who those people were.

I'm dismounting when I see a tall, strong man, with his head down, standing in front of a very beautiful black marble tomb.

He doesn't fit the place. Maybe because nothing in his posture suggests someone who is grieving, missing someone, or needing another person.

Everything about him screams that he stands alone.

Not wanting to intrude on the stranger's privacy, I take a path away from him, letting the man mourn his loss in peace.

I walk about two hundred meters and stop near the first gravestone.

"Thomas," I read mentally, "you will never be forgotten by mommy."

I look at the date and see that Thomas passed away at only nineteen. I feel my eyes well up with tears and wonder if, should they decide to end my life now, anyone would visit my grave.

The anguish I feel at the thought that even Fanya might not come close to suffocates me.

It was probably a terrible idea to come here today, after all.

Loneliness and self-pity are dangerous feelings.

I can't afford to break down. There will be no one to pick up the pieces.

Chapter 6

Rourke

About six months later

Guilt is not a foreign feeling to me. I've lived with it for a long time. Until Viona's death, I took pride in saying I never regretted anything, at least not that I could remember. That all changed. For the past four years, I've had the last day of her life etched in my memory.

I've replayed it countless times in my mind.

A stupid argument, our mutual bad temper, and then my life changed forever.

"I hope one day you can forgive me. One of us should be able to do it, at least."

I place my wife's favorite flowers—calla lilies—on her gravestone, but as always, I hesitate before leaving. I'll never accept having to leave her alone. She hated loneliness. Unlike me, she was the type who loved having people around.

I look at the cold grave and wonder if I'll ever be able to connect it with the vibrant girl who danced in the rain and liked to go out for ice cream in the dead of night.

If there were justice in this world, it would be me underground, not her. Viona had plans and dreams. A life to live.

As if sensing my mood, my phone vibrates with a message from Keiron, my best friend and Syndicate brother.

K: "Feeling like kicking some ass? Lorcan sent me to give a message to some of our newer friends."

I know he's referring to members of a new Mexican drug cartel. Apparently, they're trying to take over the market that once belonged to *Los Morales.*

For reasons unknown to us, a few months ago, our Boss, Cillian, picked a fight with those motherfuckers. I thought with the death of the two brothers who led the cartel, our involvement would be over, but apparently, even if Yerik was satisfied with the Morales' extermination, my boss is far from feeling that way.

He wants to cut the problem at the root and send a message to the emerging cartel: anyone who steps into our territory will be killed. Now, every day we're sending some Mexican souls to hell.

"Where do I meet you?"

K: "Head to warehouse five. But I should warn you that what we're about to do might not be quick. Lorcan and Cillian want this message to be unforgettable this time."

"Who's in a hurry?"

ENEMY BLOOD BEING SPILLED. Cries of pain.

The body, slowly relaxing, drained of any tension through the numbness of the mind, focused solely on fulfilling the day's mission.

I have a secret, however, that only Keiron knows. One that makes every cut of my knife into this bastard's flesh today a kind of catharsis.

For every rapist I kill, I pay tribute to Viona.

I'm not known as someone with a conscience. I kill and don't think about it again. It's not personal, it's not about revenge.

It's work.

Today, however, it's not just about following Lorcan's orders. I find pleasure in torturing the man who is not just the enemy, a member of a rival organization. He's also a womanizer.

The antagonist in front of me is someone most men would fear. He's big—at least five centimeters taller than my one meter eighty-eight—and heavy as well, with his body and face covered in tattoos, as is common among members of this new cartel, from what I've seen.

I take a step back, staring at him, and wonder what the young women he drags from their families think when they find themselves vulnerable with this son of a bitch, locked in filthy places and subjected to his twisted desires.

Fear, surely. And from what I know, that feeds the pleasure of sickos like him.

"Did I catch any of your relatives?" he asks, with the only eye he has left, his mouth empty of teeth and spitting blood. "Is that why you don't just kill me outright?"

I spin the knife in my hand.

"No, you didn't do anything to someone I know, but that's not important. What you need to understand is that I love women in general, and I take very seriously the punishment of assholes who can't keep their dick in their pants after hearing a no."

"It's not personal, fucker. They need to be broken or they wouldn't be useful for what we want. When they're sold, they have to be submissive."

I move closer and spend a few minutes making a precise cut. When I finish, two ribs are exposed.

He screams, cries, pleads.

I smile.

"What's wrong? I'm just doing my job. It's not personal. You need to be broken to serve my purpose." I point the knife at the flaccid member, already partially sliced between his thighs, and with another cut, he curses me, only to return to begging the next second. "It's amazing how pieces of shit like you, who view inflicting pain on others as something casual, scream like a baby when it's inflicted on your own flesh."

"Aren't you tired yet?" I hear Keiron ask behind me.

I know he's already killed the other two cartel members, but he let me take my time with this one, knowing I need to rid the poison from my body. I have to let it out. It's the only way to keep breathing.

He's usually with me on these longer missions and is the one who always pulls me back, because I could continue torturing this son of a bitch for days.

"Rourke, finish this up. The message has been sent. I have someone waiting for us," he says.

I know he's talking about our arrangement. I haven't touched a woman since I recovered my wife's body. As punishment, I don't allow myself to feel anyone, because she'll never be able to have the same from me again.

Desire, however, still makes my blood boil, and no amount of masturbation in the shower or in my bed at night makes it disappear.

One day, I walked into one of our clubs and saw him fucking one of the dancers.

They both noticed I was watching and didn't seem to care.

It wasn't planned. I never fucked a woman in public or had the desire to do so.

I never imagined myself as a *voyeur*, but with the arousal burning every cell in my body, I became an *enthusiastic observer*.

The arrangement has worked for years. I don't allow myself more than to watch. It will have to be enough forever.

I approach the undead hanging in front of me and, with a precise cut, slice his throat.

Then, I drop the knife on the floor, knowing a cleanup crew is already ready to take care of everything.

"Not today," I reply, turning my back and heading for the exit.

Chapter 7

Keiron

I know that with every knife wound inflicted on the half-dead Mexican, Rourke finds a new breath to keep on living.

Only someone who exists within the hell of a guilty conscience can recognize a kindred spirit.

We've been childhood friends. I don't remember a significant moment in my life when he wasn't there, and I'd do anything to ease the pain he feels.

"Rourke, finish this up. The message has been sent. I have someone waiting for us," I say, not because I'm particularly in the mood to fuck today, but because I know I need to pull him out of his rage trance, or he could keep working on the enemy for days.

It wouldn't be the first time. I was with him throughout the time he punished the man who killed Viona, his late wife. As many stab wounds as she took from her killer, it equaled the number of days Rourke spent inflicting his own pain on the bastard.

Eleven times twenty-four. A total of two hundred sixty-four hours of torture, during which he only stopped for short breaks to rest.

Yes, he spent eleven days with the man, making him pay for every second of suffering he caused Viona, and yet, from personal experience, I knew it wouldn't help. Inflicting suffering, revenge, doesn't do anything to alleviate our own hell in the long run.

The balm is temporary. It never lasts long.

"Not today," he replies, and only then do I remember that it's the anniversary of his wife's death.

That's why he was out of touch for so long this afternoon. He must have gone to the cemetery as he does on her birthday and Christmas.

"I wasn't talking about sex, you fucking pervert," I say, following him.

Yes, I was.

Usually, after missions, I like to wash away the smell of blood inside a tight pussy, but what he needs today is not to *observe* but to have someone by his side.

He stops walking.

"Nice try, but I'm going home, Keiron. I'm not in the mood to meet other brothers at one of our clubs."

I know he can't stand the looks of recognition of his pain or the useless attempts at consolation. Maybe that's why we get along so well and why working directly with Lorcan is so easy. The three of us understand that there are things beyond any chance of repair.

The fucking "everything will be okay" or "time heals" is the worst lie anyone can tell another in suffering.

Time doesn't heal.

Time makes you not remember as often, but the pain will always be there.

"It's not in our territory," I reply, and I see him raise an eyebrow.

There are few places in Boston that don't belong to an organization, but they do exist.

Neutrality is respected by all who want to live to see the sun rise the next day. In them, we can have fun without declaring a fucking war.

"What are you thinking?"

I shrug.

"Beer and pool. We don't need to talk, but I'm not leaving you alone today. You might think that's what you need, but it's not. The human mind is a fucking labyrinth, Rourke. I'll never let you get lost in it to the point of never finding your way back."

IS SHE AWARE THAT SHE'S being watched?

If I had to guess, I'd say yes. I've caught the blonde glancing over her shoulder a few times during her solitary game of pool.

I glance to the side and notice that Rourke also seems mesmerized by her.

Not that we're the only ones. Despite the place being packed with women, the girl steals all the attention.

I don't think it's just the blonde hair cascading down her back, making me want to wrap it around my fist while I fuck her from behind. Or even her sculpted body, long legs, and the ample, high-arched ass that draws the hungry gaze of the men present.

It's the complete indifference to everyone around her that makes her stand out, like a diamond among semi-precious stones. She seems trapped inside herself—or at least she did, until our first exchange of glances.

We arrived at the "neutral" bar about two hours ago. After a few beers and some rounds of pool, I saw her.

I tried not to be too obvious, even though mentally I made a pact with myself to not leave without getting her phone number.

My desire was to take her home, but I promised Rourke that we'd just go out for a beer.

"Changed your mind?" I ask when I see his undisguised interest in the woman.

He swallows hard and shakes his head, saying no, though I know him well enough to know that he wants her too.

"Not today," he repeats, "but it wouldn't be a bad idea to get her number."

He never approaches women to avoid giving the wrong impression that he'll fuck them. We both pick and our tastes always align, but it's me who introduces myself to them.

I finish my beer and set the bottle on the bar.

"I was thinking the same. She's hot. I can't let this slip by."

Chapter 8

Tulia

I feel a gaze burning into my back and I know, by intuition, that one of them is approaching me.

I have no problem with my appearance and I'm used to being coveted by men when I go out at night, but the obvious desire from the opposite sex has never interested me until now.

I was raised to be with only one man—Simeon was my first boyfriend, my first everything, and also my greatest disappointment.

Since the end of our relationship, or perhaps better said, the destruction of our engagement, I haven't been able to be with anyone else.

Not that I'm indifferent to good-looking men, but it's as if I'm stuck. My self-esteem, far beyond the physical aspect, and into the psychological, was deeply shaken by my ex-fiancé. In one fell swoop, I lost everything.

I was preparing for a second solitary game of pool when I first saw them.

Yes, not just one, but two handsome men, each with a beer in hand, staring at me as if it were just the three of us in the bar.

Normally, in a situation like this, I would be on alert. After three years working in the Organization—and even though for the last year I've been more of a decoration that my superiors weren't quite sure where to place—I've seen a lot of shit since becoming a member of the

Brotherhood, and I know that groups of men with arousal and alcohol rarely end well.

However, the two handsome men watching me don't scare me. Quite the opposite, as if there were a blessed magnet pulling us together, I can't stop glancing at them, even if discreetly, from time to time. And now that I realize one of them is very close, there's a frantic dance of butterflies in my stomach.

Maybe it's time to end my loneliness? Not that I want something long-term, but at least I could have some fun for a night.

I've had the freedom to go out and socialize since my last conversation with Sierra. I haven't received any new assignments since the failure of the first, but I think the possible death sentence was postponed.

I pretend to study a shot, but my body is fully alert to the approaching stranger. Out of the corner of my eye, I notice it's the one with almost black hair and a model-like face, with muscles that even his clothes can't disguise.

From what I've observed, they are contrasts, each hot as hell in their own way. While this one has a kind of amusement in his eyes, as if he knows exactly what I'm thinking—or wanting—the other, with a beard and a very mean look, gazes at me reluctantly. Every time I caught him looking at me, I noticed a bit of anger, as if he didn't want to do it but couldn't help himself.

"A game?" The one who came close to me asks, with an arrogance that makes him even more delicious.

I straighten my body, standing upright, and for a moment, I allow myself to study him.

It takes exactly fifteen seconds for my hormones to go wild. If from a distance he seemed handsome enough to stand out in a bar full of good-looking alpha males, now, just a few steps away, he's even better.

"I'm the solitary type," I reply, and that's one of the truest things I can say about myself these days.

I was never the life of the party, but I'm more guarded than ever. Despite this, it's tempting to flirt with the arrogant stranger.

"Or maybe you're afraid of losing."

I feel a corner of my mouth lift because I know he's teasing me, but I hide it, as I still haven't decided whether I'll let him come closer.

Without being able to control myself, my eyes follow the second man. It's the exact moment he's taking a sip of his beer, his eyes fixed on me, and I feel a shiver of desire as I notice the movement of his throat as he swallows.

"Or maybe I'm a nice person and don't want to humiliate you by beating you in front of your friend," I say, gesturing with my head beyond his shoulder.

When he smiles instead of getting offended, I realize I'm screwed because not only is he incredibly hot, but he's confident. Only a guy who knows his power wouldn't be unsettled by the irony in my voice.

"Beautiful and cheeky. I think I've found the woman of my dreams."

The urge to smile grows because he's so bold. I've never given myself the chance to flirt. I wasn't even sure until now if I knew how to do it, but I feel my body completely engaged in this innocent game between us.

"Here's the thing, gorgeous. I can't stay long today, but I need your phone number as much as I need my next breath."

He intrigues me. While he shows a lightness with his words, he has an intense and even dangerous look. Not because he makes me fear him, but that type of look that makes it clear he's a man not to be trifled with.

"You didn't even tell me your name." I venture.

"Do names matter?" he asks, with a smile that, I'm sure, makes panties fall off with a wink.

His eyes are a deep brown, like melted dark chocolate, and I feel my pulse race so furiously as if I'm facing the first man to ever flirt with me in my life.

I shiver and am almost sure he notices. Despite the brief exchange of words between us, the sexual tension is palpable.

I force myself to put my brain cells back to work again.

"Doesn't matter? So, what do you call your opponents?"

"Is that what you'll be, blonde? An *opponent*?"

I shrug.

"You're the one who offered to play with me. All I can tell you is that I never enter a competition to lose."

I see something ignite in his face like fireworks on the Fourth of July, and I quickly recognize what it is: to him, I've just become a challenge.

Before he can respond, however, a girl who must be around my age approaches me.

"Can you walk me to the bathroom? I'm not feeling well."

I look at her, certain she's mistaken me for someone else, but there's a universal silent code between women, and her look says: *follow me for your own good.*

I don't question it. I leave the cue on the table and, without saying goodbye, turn my back on the handsome guy.

"Elaine, damn it!" I hear him say, and the woman turns back, laughing.

"Go find another victim, Keiron. This one is too innocent for your poison."

As soon as we get to the bathroom, I turn to her.

"Alright. I trusted your silent message, now can you tell me what the hell is going on?"

She's very pretty. At first glance, she seems simple—brown hair and eyes, average physique—but as you start to pay attention to her features, you see she's breathtakingly beautiful.

"I'm going to assume you have enough self-confidence to come to a place like this alone."

"A place like *this*?" I repeat, playing dumb, and she raises an eyebrow in response.

Immediately, I'm on alert.

She also knows this is a neutral territory bar for the organizations. I can see it in her gaze.

"Who are you?" I ask, suspiciously.

"A good Samaritan trying to save your skin, girl. You're pretty and seem too innocent to be here."

"Alright, I'm not getting it, so I'll rephrase the question: who are those guys?"

"Men who aren't good for naïve girls. Consider today your lucky day, baby. I just saved you from getting involved with two members of the Irish syndicate."

After that, she gives me a kiss on the cheek and leaves.

I don't even know what shocks me more: whether it's that she noticed my interest in both *simultaneously*, while I thought I was hiding it well; or finding out that the men who sparked sexual attraction in me for the first time since the end of my engagement are none other than members of a rival mafia.

I leave the bathroom and head for the service entrance of the bar. When I reach it, I rush to the parking lot to get my motorcycle.

I ride like I'm being chased by the devil, and even when I get to my apartment, I'm still trembling, because if falling out of Sierra's favor didn't sign my death warrant, going to bed with an Irish mobster surely would.

Chapter 9

Rourke

Days Later

"I'm not sure I understand very well," I say to the *Boss*, while my gaze meets Keiron's, who looks as lost as I do.

If it were anyone other than the supreme boss here with us, I would have told them to fuck off by now, because I work directly with Lorcan, and the idea of receiving instructions behind his back pisses me the hell off.

However, speaking is not only Cillian, the head of the Syndicate, but also Lorcan's cousin, which means that whatever he's trying to tell us, it's to protect him.

"In an hour, Lorcan will go to meet Taisiya. It's her birthday," he says, referring to the novice girl who has become Lorcan's ward. "Hell, the Russians will definitely send a bodyguard with her. I want you to keep an eye on this guy. The girl isn't the problem. She's just a teenager, but I don't trust Yerik. Even though he's also Lorcan's cousin, the Russian Pakhan and I hate each other. Hitting Lorcan would be a way to hit me."

"With all due respect, *Boss*," Keiron interrupts. "But I don't think he would do something like that. Ruslan would never allow it."

"Logically, I agree, but I don't work with assumptions. I like to anticipate moves. I don't care about the deals between that bastard Yerik and Ruslan. My goal is to protect my blood."

"I'd like a bit more clarity in the orders, Cillian," I ask.

"Any move this bodyguard makes against Lorcan, shoot to kill."

Again, Keiron and I exchange glances, and I know we're both thinking the same thing: if there's a shootout and the novice girl gets hit, Lorcan will go insane. None of us, however, comment on it.

Who would be foolish enough to talk about the strange relationship between a Russian mafia princess—and a novice at that—and Cillian's right-hand man?

Not because we haven't talked about it, though, that any of us understand this shit.

"Rest assured, we'll keep a close watch on the guy," Keiron says, his face reflecting what I'm thinking: a fucking punishment to babysit a Russian all day.

Once we're alone in the hallway, he leans against the wall and rubs his face with both hands.

"And here I was thinking I'd enjoy the party Kellan is throwing at the club tonight."

"Instead, we're stuck babysitting a damn Russian. The day couldn't get any worse."

"What Cillian said, about it being a trap for Lorcan: if we have to shoot, protect the girl. I'll handle the bodyguard," he says.

"No, thanks. The hero that women love is you. I'd rather deal with the Russian, buddy."

WE'RE IN THE VEHICLE behind Lorcan's, in the convent parking lot, waiting for the Russian princess to leave.

Cillian had already sent a team to check the entire perimeter, but still, we're ordered to keep our exposure to a minimum.

When we notice Lorcan getting out of the car, we do the same.

I can see the novice girl walking towards him from a distance. She's beautiful, and if I had to guess, Lorcan is a beaten warrior who hasn't even realized it yet.

However, my attention on her lasts only a few seconds because it's the tall blonde woman walking a few steps behind Taisiya who captivates me.

I glance at Keiron, and when I hear a "fuck me," I know I'm not going crazy.

It's her. The blonde from the bar who ran from us, thanks to that busybody Elaine. We were both pissed about the interference and when Keiron asked the nosy one—who turns out to be Juno's best friend—what she'd said to the girl, she shrugged and said she didn't deal with mobsters, nor did she wish that on anyone.

Now, however, I realize that what might have made the woman run from the bar wasn't just because we weren't the good guys in the story, but because she had a secret of her own: she's Russian.

"Can you believe this?" Keiron asks.

"No. What could her relation be to the novice? They don't look physically alike."

And then, as if our thoughts cleared at the same time, we stare at each other.

"Fuck, she's the bodyguard," Keiron says, and to confirm, we hear Lorcan's ward say:

"Could you excuse us, Tulia? Don't take it the wrong way. I know you've been assigned to keep an eye on me while I'm with Lorcan, but today is my birthday and I haven't seen him in a year. I want some privacy."

She hasn't noticed us yet and doesn't seem willing to leave them alone. If she were a man, I'd kick his ass because only an idiot wouldn't see that they need some time alone. But besides not hitting women, I don't want to have more contact with her than necessary.

I can't deny that I would have liked, before knowing her identity, to have her join our three-way meetings. She's gorgeous and aroused me like no one else has since Viona, but now that we know who she is, that's out of the question.

With a grunt, she steps away from them.

When she lifts her head and sees us, her eyes widen, and an adorable flush spreads across her face and neck.

If I were paranoid, I'd think that the fucking Pakhan orchestrated the bar meeting, trying to insert a spy into our midst, but besides the fact that we were in neutral territory, she was the one who decided to leave that night. So, I can only think that it was pure chance that created that situation.

Tulia—yes, now we know the blonde's name—doesn't seem willing to back down even after Taisiya's warning. Not even when Lorcan puts an arm around his ward's shoulders, guiding her to his vehicle, does the blonde get the hint.

"You're coming with them," he says, nodding his head in our direction.

Without waiting for a response, he makes Taisiya get in the back seat and follows her, closing the door and leaving the blonde outside.

"And I'm hating the mission Cillian gave us. Damn, this is going to be fun," Keiron says.

I step in front of him, turning my back to the Russian.

"Don't even think about it. Delicious or not, she's the enemy, Keiron. We need to keep an eye on her."

"Yes, we do, but that doesn't mean we can't enjoy the time together."

Chapter 10

Tulia

I fake a calmness that I'm far from feeling. In reality, my legs are shaking like jelly as millions of theories race through my mind simultaneously.

In the daylight, the second man is even more intimidating. In fact, both of them are now that the flirting factor has been thrown to hell.

My heart is beating so fast I'm afraid they might hear it; before I have a heart attack, I decide to spill:

"Did you know who I was? Was that night at the bar a game?"

The angry one crosses his arms over his chest, and every blessed muscle is outlined by his jacket.

It takes me a while to realize he's speaking to me, as I'm somewhat hypnotized by his body.

"What exactly would have been a game?" he asks, and I feel my face burning.

However, I'm not going to let them toy with me.

"You..." I say, looking at the one who approached me at the bar and deliberately ignoring the handsome asshole. "I want to know if when you approached me at the bar, you knew I was a Russian soldier. Was that some kind of mission?"

They look at each other, and to my surprise, even the nasty one almost seems to smile.

"I'm Keiron, Tulia," the one who spoke to me at the bar says. "As for your question, it was kind of a mission, yes, love, but not the type you're thinking. Now, for obvious reasons, it won't happen. So, if you're done with your interrogation, move your Russian ass to the car. We don't have all day, and Lorcan wants to give his girl a happy day."

Before I can respond, the other man circles the vehicle, opens the back door, and sits down. Then, Keiron places his hand on the small of my back and guides me to do the same. In the blink of two eyes, I'm wedged between them in the back seat.

To my surprise, the other man, who still hasn't introduced himself, fastens my seatbelt as if I were incapable of doing it myself.

"What's your name?" I ask him, only to regret it two seconds later.

By his expression when he looks at me, he's not in the mood for conversation.

"We're not friends and we won't be, Tulia. Why should my name matter to you?"

"Do you have pre-rehearsed lines?" I mock, refusing to let him see that I'm embarrassed. "Because it's almost the same thing Keiron told me the other night at the bar."

"Let me tell you something, *soldier*," the nameless one says, ignoring my sarcasm and emphasizing my role as an enemy. "That day, Keiron wanted to take you home. We didn't know you were Russian, let alone a member of the Organization. Today, we're here to watch you. One wrong move and you'll be dead."

The threat should scare me, but I must be really crazy because the only thing I feel is the hair on both of their arms standing up, since I'm pressed against both of them.

I lift my chin and stare at him, making a scowl, even though I don't believe for a second that they could harm me.

I'm a bodyguard for Taisiya, a Russian mafia princess. It doesn't matter that within the Organization, at the moment, due to Sierra's anger towards me, I'm worth less than a five-cent coin. As long as I'm guarding Anastacia's sister, I'm protected.

"I could not want to kill Lorcan, but one of you. Or both. Have you thought about that? I have a volatile temper. I'm explosive, and if you keep threatening me, I might end up deciding to embark on a suicide mission."

To my dismay, Keiron laughs.

"No death threats, sweetheart. Behave yourself, and at the end of the day, we'll give you a ride home."

"I don't need a ride. As soon as I make sure Taisiya is at the convent, I'll leave on my own."

"As you wish, love."

"Don't call me 'love'. I'm the enemy, not one of your conquests."

Again he smiles, but this time he brings his mouth very close to my ear.

"No, you're not one of *ours* to conquer. And that's a shame, baby. Something tells me that I, you, and Rourke would have a lot of fun together."

I feel my pulse go wild, wondering if I heard that right.

He said "one of *ours* to conquer," as if they were a team?

Jesus, just thinking that these two might share a woman in a room at the same time makes my body ignite.

I turn to look at the other side, intending to check out Rourke.

No. The angry giant doesn't seem like the sharing type.

While Keiron wears the conqueror persona like a second skin, the other man acts as if he's above the rest of humanity and nothing could shake him or make his blood boil.

As if sensing that he's under my scrutiny, he, who had been looking out the window, turns in his seat to stare at me.

For whole seconds, he looks at me intensely, his blue eyes deep as if trying to uncover all my secrets. What I see on his face contradicts everything he's said so far about considering me an enemy. I'm not an idiot; he desires me.

Throwing caution to the wind, as a sort of test, I let my tongue glide over my lower lip.

My whole body tingles as his gaze darkens, focusing on my lips.

That's right, I'm not crazy. He might be better at hiding it than his friend, but just like I thought that day at the bar, he wants me too.

I feel a shift in the seat beside me. A solid chest pressing against my arm and warm lips against my left earlobe.

"He likes to watch, Tulia," Keiron whispers. "Just watch."

After dropping that bombshell, as if they had coordinated, both of them turn back to their respective windows.

I lean back in the seat and close my eyes, trying to erase the image he hinted at from my mind, but it's no use.

The thought of being touched by Keiron while Rourke watches will be my dirtiest, secret fantasy for a long time to come.

Chapter 11

Tulia

"You're not going to risk your tough-guy pose by relaxing for a few minutes," Keiron whispers in my ear.

He's done this a lot, using the excuse that the music is too loud inside the club — yes, *club*.

The damned nun decided to celebrate her coming of age in a *nightclub* owned by the Irish mafia.

I try to suppress a shiver caused by his proximity, but I think he notices how my body vibrates with the slightest contact, as he smiles.

"The air conditioning is strong in here," I explain, and his smile widens.

Damn cocky Irishman.

I've been watching the enemies and the Russian princess enjoy a private party for hours, which seems like part of a parallel reality.

How, in heaven, the Pakhan allowed this, I'll never understand.

The tension I feel at this moment, however, has nothing to do with being in enemy territory, but with my past.

Watching women who can't be much older than me enjoying life as if there were no tomorrow, I wonder what the hell I was thinking when I decided to get married right out of adolescence.

I never experienced any of this — parties, fun — and it's not just because my upbringing was strict, but because I existed solely for the next breath of Simeon.

I catch a movement out of the corner of my eye and when I look over, I realize Rourke has a woman almost throwing herself at him.

I know it's stupid of me, but it annoys me.

They throw themselves at both of them like flies to honey.

I can't condemn them because if we weren't who we are, I wouldn't mind getting to know one of them better. "*Or both simultaneously,*" a wicked voice intrudes in my mind.

No, both would be impossible, even if I were a tramp capable of such adventures, because Keiron said Rourke likes to *watch*.

I can't stop thinking about it. He set my body on fire with that information.

The woman touches Rourke's arm and he doesn't move, doesn't try to pull away, but he's not flirting either.

Why just watch?

Jesus, a man like that just watching seems like a waste.

I once read a little about fetishes and know that this is called *voyeurism*. The excitement caused by observing someone or even couples. It usually has a sexual connotation.

It's a puzzle I can't piece together. Rourke seems like the type who turns a woman inside out in bed. I swear, the man could make a lady reach climax just with those bad-boy eyes, so why not join in the fun?

And besides, how does Keiron allow his friend to be a spectator in their encounters? My experience with men is limited to Simeon, but I don't need to be a sex expert to know I'm dealing with two alpha males who like to mark their territory.

My God, just a few hours out of my comfort zone and they're about to blow my mind.

I tried not to think about them after Elaine, the woman at the bar, informed me that they were Irish mafiosos, but since I thought I'd never see them again, I allowed myself to fantasize about both.

However, *one at a time.*

Rourke turns and catches me in the act of coveting him, just as I feel Keiron's hand on my hip.

"Let's dance, baby. If you get any more tense, you'll split in two. You're like a taut guitar string."

I spin to face him, only to realize I made a mistake because now our mouths are just inches apart.

"I didn't come here to have fun; I came to look after Taisiya," I insist, even though the naughty nun has disappeared with Lorcan to the back of the room.

I lost sight of both of them about five minutes ago.

"You know very well they need some time together, Tulia. I swear I won't bite you, unless you ask me to. It's just a dance."

"And kill me?" I provoke, God knows why.

"Oh no, you're too pretty to die...," he pauses, "today, at least."

I feel a shiver that's not from fear, but also not just from desire.

I don't think Keiron is threatening me. In his way, it's a type of flirtation, but I know with every drop of blood running through my body that he would be capable of killing me in the name of the Syndicate. I represent the enemy.

And the reverse, would it be true? I've never had to hurt anyone since joining the Brotherhood, despite knowing how to defend myself very well. But could I take a life — his or Rourke's — if necessary?

I have no answer for that.

"You think too much, blonde."

I cross my arms in front of my chest and confront him:

"I don't buy this easygoing attitude of yours. You're not fooling me."

He raises an eyebrow, looking surprised.

"I don't know what you're talking about."

I step closer, and this time, I'm the one whispering in his ear:

"You want me, but you also see me as the enemy. Don't try to manipulate me. I'm not like those girls drooling over you, desperate to be *the chosen one*."

The hand that was on my hip moves down to my ass, grabbing it entirely, and I'm torn between kicking his balls or positioning myself so he can hold me better.

I don't have time to decide because warm lips nip at my earlobe.

"Yes, you're right to think I'd be capable of killing you if you gave me a reason," he says, guessing what I was thinking a few moments ago, "but if I had the choice, I'd rather have you spread out on my dining table, your thighs on my shoulders, screaming my name while I suck on your clit until you fill my mouth with your orgasm."

I'm so dazed by the unexpected verbal attack that instead of trying to pull away, I lean against his arm.

"You can't say things like that to me, Keiron. You know nothing will ever happen between us, and besides, I don't..."

"Don't what? Don't come hard? Then you're with the wrong guy, baby."

"I don't have a boyfriend," I say, even though it's none of his business.

He pulls back a little, but we're still very close.

I don't even realize what's happening until I feel a wall at my back and see that the people at the party are no longer visible.

The man is magical, he must be. He moved me without me even knowing what was happening.

He holds my chin and forces me to look at him.

"I want a taste of you."

"No," I say, feeling my pulse quicken. "You've lost your mind. We're in public."

My God, what did I just say?

I gave the impression that if it weren't for the audience, I'd give in!

"And wouldn't you?" the damned naughty voice mocks.

He runs his thumb over my lower lip, and I feel my legs turn to cooked spaghetti. I've never experienced this kind of seduction and have no idea how to act.

I mean, my rational side knows I should push him away, because the man is dangerous to me not only because he probably swaps women as quickly as he changes underwear, but also because he's from the enemy mafia.

The bad news is that my rational side no longer commands a damn thing, and when his rough, thick finger brushes against the flesh of my mouth again, I open it, letting him slide the tip between my lips.

"Suck."

Jesus, he said that as if he's telling me to...

I don't have the courage to complete the thought and just shake my head, signaling no.

"Let me see, Tulia. Stick that tasty tongue out, baby."

I take a breath, trying to remember that I need to breathe.

"I thought it was Rourke who liked to watch." I try to break the mood.

"Yes, he watches and I do, but I can't fuck you here and you can't go home with me, so I want to imagine that delicious mouth around my cock. I want to know what it feels like to have your wet lips sucking me."

If it were any other guy, I'd send him to hell and push him away, but he's not being vulgar. The man is too sexy.

"Suck."

This time, instead of resisting, the bad girl inside me decides to put on a show, so I let my tongue slip out and, with my eyes closed, trace circles on his thumb.

I hear a low growl and when I open my eyes, Keiron is watching me as if he wants to rip my clothes off and devour me right there.

Without removing his finger from my lips, his mouth drops to my neck, nipping at the sensitive flesh, while one of his legs presses between mine.

I let him stay, even though I know I should tell him to stop, telling myself it will just be a taste of him to spice up my fantasies.

His teeth are now nipping at me roughly, and I moan, crazed with a need I don't even quite understand.

When I open my eyes, I see Rourke just a few steps away, focused on us.

I can't see his face, but his posture is tense, like a predator about to pounce on its prey, and at that moment, what goes through my mind is that I'd like to be his prey.

I want to be between the two of them.

The thought scares me, and I push Keiron away as if he were a snake that had bitten me.

He doesn't look at me in shock when I push him. On the contrary, he seems lost in himself, as if he hadn't meant to go this far.

"Don't touch me again," I warn. "I said I'd kill if necessary. I'd also kill any of you. Don't doubt it."

Chapter 12

Keiron

I watch the cleaning crew drag the Mexican bodies to the mass grave, knowing the routine by heart. They will be dissolved in acid until nothing remains but bones.

The only way for the people we send to hell to be identified is if we want them to be; otherwise, there will be no evidence left.

When Cillian wants to send a message, we take a son of a bitch for sampling and display the dead body in all the glory of the work of art we've made on him, revealing to our enemies what their fate will be if they cross the line and invade our territory.

I like what I do. I never wanted to be anything other than serving the Syndicate, but sometimes I get tired of this daily war. There isn't a damn day of rest for our minds. We're always looking over our shoulders, and the same applies to our enemies.

Blood spilled on a permanent basis. Fights, pain.

Both I and any other member have been stabbed or shot. Coming home with a damaged part of the body is somewhat expected.

I've always seen it as normal, even routine, but for the first time, I wonder what it's like to live in a world like this for someone like Tulia.

I don't need to be a fortune teller to know she hasn't been in this life for long. Even before having her researched, which I did after the night we spent together at the club, I had a sense of her background. The only piece I'm missing is understanding why she went from being an ordinary young woman, who was about to get married in a month, to a member of the Russian Organization.

The ex-fiancé, also a soldier of the Brotherhood, hasn't married yet, and strangely maintains a good relationship with her family, who lives in Kentucky, while, as far as I could verify, Tulia has never returned there.

I found out that she is hated by the wife of one of Pakhan's trusted men, which means her chances of making a career in the Organization are nil, but what intrigues me is the certainty that she doesn't belong to any mafia. I'm talking about *heart*.

I saw in her eyes that she's never killed anyone. No matter how tough she thinks she is, there's no typical emptiness in Tulia of those who have lost part of their humanity, for whom taking a life doesn't steal a night's sleep.

No, the girl still has a lot inside her, and even knowing I shouldn't get involved, as it's not my problem, she managed to pull me from my usual indifference. I don't care about other people's dramas.

I feel a presence beside me, and even without looking, I know it's Rourke. When you've known someone your whole life, you guess even the echo of their footsteps, just as I also know what he's thinking.

He's barely spoken to me since the night at the club, and the reason is that he thinks I crossed an imaginary line by getting involved with Tulia, putting both our lives at risk.

In a mutual, silent agreement, there haven't been any more encounters with women since she started serving as security for the nun-girl.

It wasn't for lack of opportunity, it was a lack of will.

Once a week, the blonde is around us, and there's nothing we can do about it. She takes orders from Taisiya, and we, from Cillian, to keep an eye on her.

The feeling when we're all three together is like being inside a pressure cooker about to explode. The sexual tension is palpable, and even Rourke, who usually keeps himself apart, above any human emotion, can't seem to take his eyes off her.

"It's not going to happen, Keiron," he says, and I don't need to ask what he's talking about. We both know.

There's something about the woman that has activated the hunter in us. We've never had to make an effort to attract female attention, but the Russian, since the only night we had more contact, remains distant, even though Taisiya leaves her alone with us.

The feigned indifference makes the desire to possess her multiply infinitely.

I don't respond. I start to gather my knives — the tools used today in the massacre against the Mexicans.

"I'm not going to let you kill yourself just because you're horny. You know how this will end. Either you end up dead by Pakhan's hands or Cillian's."

I clean the blood off my favorite knife.

"She's just a girl, Rourke. She's not a spy or a high-ranking member. And if I can give a hint, she never will be."

"What does that mean?"

I'm not surprised by his interest. Despite keeping away from Tulia when she comes with Lorcan's girl, I've known him long enough to realize that the blonde affects him a lot too.

I quickly recount what I discovered about her history.

"Are you telling me she's hated by Leonid's wife?"

"Yes. I don't know the details because those fucked-up Russians are tighter than clams, and it's hard to get information, but from everything I've discovered, it's a miracle she's still alive. So, if you think Tulia was sent to get something from us, seduce or anything like that, you're mistaken. I think they don't know what to do with her, just like they don't know what to do with Taisiya."

"Who's the ex-fiancé?"

"Simeon Morozov. An idiot. It's the only explanation for letting a woman like her slip away."

"People who hear you might think you're husband material. It's not like you're looking for a serious relationship."

"The fact that I'm too damaged to stay with someone forever doesn't mean I can't recognize a good girl when I see one. A man who had Tulia and lost her can only be a fool."

I see on his face that he agrees but won't admit it.

"Find someone. Relieve that damn tension, but forget the Russian. Tell your dick to look the other way. She's not worth it."

"Are you going to do the same with yours? Because I don't believe for a second you wouldn't love to have her with us. We're too similar. The challenge pushes us to the limit, and Tulia is the most challenging conquest we've had in years."

His phone rings, and from the conversation, I know it's Lorcan.

After he hangs up, I see him run both hands over his face.

"We need to go meet him," he says. "Once again, we'll be babysitting the blonde."

"The blizzard will get worse. I was planning to head straight home."

"The nun shouldn't be out too long. Let's get this over with."

"IT'S GOING TO SNOW even more," Tulia says, looking agitated.

It's rare for her to take the initiative to speak, especially about the weather.

"And what's the problem with that? You live in Boston," Rourke responds, making it surreal, because I can count on one hand how many times he's spoken to her. After the conversation earlier today, I thought he'd keep his distance.

"I don't like snow," she says simply, but it's not just the statement; it's how her voice sounds distressed that catches my attention.

"Some trauma or something?" I ask.

She's squeezed between us on the couch, and unlike the previous times we had physical contact, even if very light, this time it was Tulia who took the initiative to stay so close.

Maybe because the gym is packed with Irish fighters and, somehow, she feels more comfortable with the *evil* already known.

"I found out my fiancé was cheating on me on a day when it was snowing heavily. I caught him in the act at our new house. I mean, the house we were going to live in."

"I don't know anything about your relationship, but he's an idiot for cheating on you."

She looks at me, and her cheeks turn red, but when she speaks, it's not about my statement:

"My hatred for snow isn't just about the scene I witnessed, but also because of the memory of running for miles in the blizzard. I couldn't stop running. I left my whole life behind. I associate snow with pain."

She's spoken more to us in this unexpected conversation than in weeks, and I realize Rourke is as shocked as I am, but before we can say anything, the door opens and Taisiya comes out of the private gym with Lorcan behind her.

Chapter 13

Tulia

As if God took pity on me after the foolishness I spoke, the door opens and Lorcan and Taisiya come out of the private gym room.

Jesus, why did I confess, of all people, to those two, who are not just complete strangers but, beyond that, *enemies*, about my snow phobia?

I walk toward the head nun as if she were my lifeline, which, in a way, isn't entirely untrue.

I've been avoiding Rourke and Keiron like the devil avoids the cross, each time Anastacia's sister meets with her Irish mobster. Since I'm forced to stay for hours in their "company," if we can call it that, I spend my time fiddling with my phone like a teenager or reading on my Kindle, pretending not to notice all that health and testosterone around me.

They haven't made any effort to approach me, and even Keiron, with his charming ways, has kept his distance, which, I must admit, hasn't done my ego any favors.

God, when will these meetings between Taisiya and Lorcan end? Why don't they just start World War III and come out already? Because not even the most gullible person in the world would believe that Maxim's sister-in-law spends hours locked up with the Irishman just chatting.

While their situation remains unresolved, I'll have to keep coming and trying to calm my hormones.

Maybe I should just go out and find someone, anyone, and fulfill all my fantasies.

I look at my "boss," who seems satisfied and happy.

I followed orders, doing my job convincing Sierra to accept the trap job Leonid offered—and as *a reward*, I get this punishment.

I must be the unluckiest person in the world to, instead of pursuing a full-blown career as a mobster, end up babysitting a novice.

Did Sierra have to be so bitter? Damn it!

The problem isn't even the novice-girl or her superhero. It's me who can't recognize myself every time I'm forced to meet the two Irish giants.

I'm getting used to them. To both of them.

How stupid can this be?

I never imagined I could be interested in a man again after what happened with Simeon, and certainly didn't expect to be interested in both of them at the same time, because if you want a synonym for "whatever," look at them.

"I'm fine alone. I just need to move on with my life and advance within the Organization," I tell myself.

"The beautiful giants are enemies, damn hormones," I say to myself as I look back and catch them watching me.

I shake my head, trying to clear my mind, but it's no use. I think I'm obsessed.

"Lorcan is taking us today," Taisiya says.

"Why?"

She shrugs.

"I want to have a little more chat with my *protector*," she says, putting irony into the last word.

"You shouldn't speak like that. Your protector is your brother-in-law. Maxim would go crazy if he heard that," I say quietly so that only she can hear.

"Don't be picky, Tulia. I only leave the convent once a week."

I feel a pang of sympathy.

"Tired of it? Why don't you ask to leave for good?"

"I'll only do that when I remember everything from the past. Living in the dark is frightening."

"Alright," I concede because she always wins me over with her sweetness, "I'll go with you."

"Um... no. Actually, I want to talk privately with Lorcan. Go with the guys," she says, pointing to the bodyguards who have been stealing my sleep. "They'll take you to the convent, and you can check if I arrive safely."

I look at the men, and they stare back at me without smiling.

"Go, Tulia. They won't harm you. They're under Lorcan's orders."

I take a deep breath. My hesitation has nothing to do with fear, but with how both men make my heart race.

I look at her with my jaw clenched and very tempted to call Maxim and report her rebelliousness, but I decide to file the report later.

"They've announced an out-of-season snowstorm, Taisiya. We need to leave quickly."

"We're big girls now, Tulia. We'll be fine. See you at the convent in half an hour."

I give her a forced smile. There's nothing more I can do but give in, because I don't want to earn the hatred of another Organization wife, which I know will happen if Anastacia finds out I upset her sister.

What I had no idea about was that the ride would change my life forever.

THE STREETS ARE IMPASSABLE. I don't think I've ever seen so much snow in my life, and it keeps falling.

Since early morning, they've been covered in ice because it's been snowing for several days, and, of course, there was the announcement of the damned snowstorm, but I never imagined such chaos.

No matter how well-maintained the transportation department is, driving has become impossible.

Usually, when I go out in the car with them, there's a driver guiding and I sit between the two. Today, it's just me, Rourke, and Keiron, and I'm sitting up front with the grumpy one driving.

I try to control the automatic urge to tap my foot on the car floor, but I'm too nervous and before I realize it, I'm almost rhythmically tapping on the mat.

Then, a huge hand grips my thigh, making me jump and then freeze in place.

"Calm down. I'm not going to let anything happen to you," Rourke says, and that's the kindest thing he's said since we met. "Why all this panic?"

I shrug and look outside, embarrassed.

"I don't know. Seeing so much snow makes me feel like I'm suffocating. I must be crazy."

"There's nothing crazy about it. I also hate snow," Keiron says.

"Bad for us then, living in Boston. Maybe we should move to California," I joke, feigning calm. "It looks like the end of times."

Nothing can be seen outside the window, and all I want is to close my eyes and wake up in my warm, safe bed.

"We need to make a decision," Rourke says, looking at Keiron through the rearview mirror.

"What?" I ask, panicked. "What are you talking about?"

"Continuing to drive in this weather is suicide, Tulia," Keiron explains, as if talking to a child.

"Don't condescend to me. You can't be that much older than me."

"How old are you?"

"Almost twenty-four," I reply.

"I'm twenty-eight, and Rourke is about to turn thirty. You owe us obedience."

I hold back a smile while rolling my eyes. I know what he's doing: trying to calm me down with jokes.

Without a doubt, Keiron is the most charming mobster I've ever met.

The cell phone rings, and when I see it's Taisiya, I go on high alert.

My good God, please let nothing have happened to her.

"Hi, Taisiya."

"Tulia, are you okay?"

"Define okay. I don't consider being in the middle of a snowstorm a nice place to be, princess."

"Don't be a pain. You'll need to be as sweet as a jar of honey today for them to be nice to you too."

"What?"

"I told Ana I'm going to Lorcan's house. We can't keep driving in this weather, and neither can you. I'm really sorry about this, Tulia."

"No, wait. I can't go with them, Taisiya. Where are you?"

"Almost at Lorcan's house. I'll ask the guys to bring you here too."

"No, I don't want to stay there. I want to go home."

"Don't be selfish, Tulia. Insisting they drop you off there will put everyone's lives at risk. If you're worried about the guys treating you well, Lorcan will talk to them. Don't worry."

She hangs up before I can respond, and my hand trembles as I grip the phone.

I haven't even recovered from our conversation when one of their phones starts ringing. This time, however, it's on speaker, and I hear Lorcan's voice.

"Yes, boss," Rourke says.

"Let her stay wherever she wants," Lorcan says.

"There's no such option anymore, Lorcan. All the streets are closed."

"Alright. Then bring her to my building. There are several empty apartments."

"Um... boss..." now Keiron responds "we won't be able to reach your building."

"What are you planning then?"

"Head to my apartment."

"Are you okay with this, Tulia?" Taisiya asks, and I feel like swearing.

"I have no choice, "boss lady"— I say with irony. "Between freezing to death and staying with the enemy, I'd choose the first option, but I'm not ready to say goodbye to this world just yet."

"Alright, take care, kids" Lorcan says and hangs up.

A heavy silence falls inside the car, and if I could guess, I think each of us is lost in our own thoughts about how the coming days will be.

Chapter 14

Tulia

With great difficulty, we arrived at Keiron's apartment, and the moment he finally parked in the covered garage, I could only thank God for having the sense not to ride a motorcycle today; otherwise, it would be ruined since when I stay with Taisiya, I leave it outside the convent.

Inside the elevator, I feel like the space is tiny, which is absurd. In reality, it's huge; it could fit about ten people. It feels more like a freight elevator. However, I think the fact that I'm so tense around them gives me the impression that we're crammed together like oranges in a tight box.

It's not an unpleasant feeling, I must confess. It's comforting to have Keiron and Rourke in the middle of the snowstorm. If I were alone, I'd probably have panicked.

When the elevator finally reaches its destination, I look around, surprised to see that the entire floor belongs to Keiron. We've already exited the elevator.

And it's not just that. It looks more like an industrial warehouse, all open and very large for a single guy.

I came ready to hate the place and the company because I don't know how I'm going to survive having my two sexual fantasy avatars within reach for days on end, but I'm in love with his home.

From the black leather sofas to the iron details, like the dining table legs, to the kitchen that's visible as soon as we leave the elevator.

Still, I'm nervous.

My anxiety isn't because I think they would force me into anything. I trust what Taisiya said: they will take good care of me. Lorcan would never allow them to do anything that would upset his girl, and after a few weeks, which turned into months of interaction, I kind of formed an unplanned friendship with the little nun. The roles reversed: I went from protector to protected among the Irish wolves.

The only problem is I don't like playing Little Red Riding Hood. The character once fit me. Now, not so much.

"Make yourself at home," Keiron says, as if sensing I want to turn around and leave. "The bedrooms are on the second floor. The first one to the left of the stairs is mine. You can choose any other."

Strangely, he also seems uncomfortable, and only then do I realize that I'm not the only one feeling extremely awkward.

"I don't want to be a bother."

"None of us chose this situation," Rourke says, always sounding like a steamroller. "Let's try not to kill each other during this time together. The snow should stop in a couple of days."

He turns his back to us and heads for the stairs, showing me that he's already familiar with the place.

Do they bring women here for... um... *Jesus, I don't even know what to call it.*

Sex games? Threesome?

No, it's not a threesome, because in that case, Rourke would have to be actively involved.

Yes, I've researched everything I could find about threesomes.

Who can blame me? The guys are as hot as hell, and Keiron dropped that bit of information about Rourke being a *voyeur.* Any woman with blood running through her veins would be curious.

When I look at Keiron, I notice I've been caught red-handed in the middle of dirty thoughts, as his gaze has darkened, the initial formality replaced by something closer to hunger.

I feel a shiver run through my body and to cover it up, I cross my arms around myself, pretending to be cold.

It's a horrible lie, of course, because the apartment is warm and the temperature is lovely.

"We never play here," he says, and I'm sure, from the tone, that he's not referring to card games or any other innocent fun. "Everyone has skeletons in their closet, Tulia. I have mine too. And rules. We must never forget the rules."

Like Rourke, he starts walking toward the stairs.

"What kind of rules are you talking about?" I ask before I can stop myself.

He turns back and stares at me.

"Nothing stays inside me except for memories of a good fuck. Feelings are off the table. It's just pleasure, Tulia. With me, it will always be just pleasure, so bringing them home would give a false impression of what I want."

I get the message quickly. By being forced to come into the same environment as the three of us, in his mind, I've put myself in a safe zone because he doesn't want to share his private life with me. Being here has made me untouchable.

I'm left not knowing what to say, and he turns and starts walking again.

"Keiron?"

He stops again.

"Do you need something?"

I didn't think so. I've been fine during these solitary years, without company. Now, though, I feel anxiety growing inside me, the absence of something I can't even name increasing more and more.

"You said you hate snow too. I know the reason for my phobia. And yours?"

He has his hands in the back pockets of his jeans, in a falsely languid pose, as I can feel his tension.

When I think he won't answer, he finally says:

"My only sister killed herself on a snowy day."

I wasn't expecting that, and I'm increasingly convinced that what the two men show on the surface has nothing to do with their true *selves*. Both carry a lot of weight inside them.

"Can I ask what happened?"

"She got involved with a guy thirty years older. Our uncle, mom's brother. I killed him. She loved him and committed suicide the next day. She was only sixteen at the time."

After delivering the terrible information, he leaves. This time, for good.

Chapter 15

Tulia

I enter the first empty room I find and lean against the door with my eyes closed, still trying to absorb the impact of Keiron's revelation.

He feels responsible for his sister's death because by killing their uncle, he drove her to suicide, but from where I stand, what he did was try to protect her from an abuser—a blood relative.

God, what must it be like to carry something like that on your shoulders? To sleep and wake up knowing that your actions destroyed someone's life?

The question remains unanswered because when I open my eyes again, I come face to face with Rourke wearing nothing but black boxer briefs.

I try very hard to look away, but I can't. The man looks like a mountain of chiseled muscle.

It's not just his defined abs, powerful thighs, or the intuition that having those arms restraining me would be the best prison in the world, but because he's a monument. From his sensational body to the tattoos that trace every inch of his skin—not to mention his piercing blue eyes—Rourke is a sight to behold.

"This room is already taken. Choose another one, Russian," he growls, with his usual bad mood, though his eyes don't send me the same message as his lips.

No, if I could guess, I'd say he wants me to stay. In fact, if I were a bit more self-confident, I'd say he's itching to throw me on that bed, the same dirty thoughts that fill my mind being shared by his.

I force myself to wake up to reality.

"I didn't do it on purpose. Keiron said I could choose any room."

"This one is mine. You're not welcome."

This annoys me because even though he has a hellish temper and I already know he doesn't actively participate in his friend's games with the girls, I'm not an idiot. The physical attraction between us is mutual.

I cross my arms over my chest.

"Maybe the problem is the opposite, huh? I'm *very* welcome, but unfortunately for you, besides being an enemy to me, I'm not attracted to bad-tempered people."

"Liar."

With that simple word—very true, by the way—he manages to set my blood boiling.

His eyes gleam dangerously and when he takes a step forward, I can't help but admire his body.

A shiver of anticipation runs through me as he gets only half a meter away. I should open the door and leave, but I don't move.

I try to look away from his face, sure that, from the heat I feel, my cheeks must be flushed, which will end up betraying me.

The desire he evokes in me is so great that it feels like my body is dehydrated; I lick my lips because I think if I don't, they'll crack.

I didn't anticipate that he would continue coming toward me, and now I can't even draw my next breath. Rourke practically presses me against the door.

My treacherous eyes roam over him and I'd like to say it's because I'm paying attention to his next move, ready to defend myself if necessary, but that would be a big, round lie.

I'm eager for him to touch me. Aside from the moment he placed his hand on my thigh in the car to calm me down, Rourke has only brushed against me accidentally.

I know what Keiron said about him only looking, and I've concluded, even though it seems impossible given his beauty, that he's celibate.

The naughty girl in me wants him to break that rule with me.

"Isn't the distance between us a bit too short according to your own principles?" I ask, breathlessly.

His breathing is not normal either and I can see from his features that he's fighting an internal war.

"Touch me," I silently plead, even knowing it would be madness.

The urge to reach out and feel his stubble on my fingertips is almost painful, but I remain still.

Rourke exudes danger from every cell of his body. His nostrils flare every time he inhales.

I shiver all over when, like Keiron often does, his lips move closer to my earlobe.

"You might be only a few years younger than me, but believe me when I say that compared to what I've lived through, you're just a little girl, Tulia."

Despite the intimacy of the situation, the words are loaded with irony, making me feel like a fool. He's laughing at me.

Without thinking clearly, I splay my hands on his chest, trying to push him away. The contact generates a jolt between our skins and I immediately withdraw them. To my surprise, Rourke takes them back the next second and places them again on his own skin.

He doesn't say anything, but his eyes show me what he wants, and even though I'm insecure, I let my hands travel over his muscular chest.

He doesn't divert his gaze and my legs turn to jelly. The heat against my palms makes me want to touch him all over, makes me desire things I've never even considered doing with a stranger.

I feel feverish, needy, and now my nails graze his rigid flesh, eager to make him *feel*.

But feel what?

Desire? The same need I have?

I don't know the answer to that, just that I want Rourke to react to me.

"Is the rule one-sided? You don't touch, but you can be touched?"

I don't even know how I had the courage to ask something like that, but the truth is, I don't have a functioning neuron at this moment.

His scent is making my body sing like a tuned violin. The masculinity in Rourke is so intense, primitive, that it's as if I'm trapped in a magnetic field.

"Aren't you going to answer?"

He moves closer, his face near enough that I can feel the warmth of his breath.

I sense he's going to kiss me, and a pleasant warmth of anticipation spreads through my body.

"Rourke, dinner in half an hour?" We hear Keiron's voice from outside the room, and immediately, he pulls away from me as if waking from a trance.

"Half an hour sounds good," he replies, still staring at me.

However, I know the moment is lost. Whatever was about to happen will no longer occur.

Dying of embarrassment for practically offering myself to him, I turn to leave the room, hand on the doorknob.

I don't get to open it because a warm body presses mine against the wood.

"The rule applies to both sides. I haven't touched a woman since my wife died and I haven't let anyone touch me either."

Oh my God. He's a widower.

Now the pieces are falling into place. Rourke is celibate because he still loves his deceased wife.

Determined to salvage whatever is left of my dignity, I open the door. He doesn't move from behind me, but he doesn't stop me either. The maneuvering space I have is minimal, but the embarrassment of having exposed myself so much makes me resolute.

I flee, and this time, when I enter the next room, I'm sure that I'm alone.

He suffers for the love of his late wife, while I was thinking of making him break the rules he probably created in her honor.

I enter the bathroom, determined to stay away from him as much as possible.

Rourke is beautiful and entirely desirable, but I won't be the one to interfere between a man in love and the memory of his deceased wife.

Chapter 16

Tulia

"Thanks for the clothes," I say as I enter the kitchen. I seriously considered staying locked in my room for the rest of the night, praying that the snowstorm would pass by morning.

The only problem with that plan is that I'm starving, and I get incredibly cranky if I go too long without eating.

The cowardly Tulia is easily outmatched by the hungry Tulia. Unlike women who pretend not to have an appetite around guys, I eat as heartily as any of them and have no intention of starving myself just to avoid facing the two Irishmen again.

Keiron is fiddling with something on the stove and turns to look at me.

I thought he might tease me when he saw me.

When I came out of the bathroom, I saw that someone had left a pair of sweatpants, a black boxer brief, and a T-shirt on my bed. The intention was good, but I had to borrow the bathrobe's belt to keep the pants up on my waist.

I also had to tie a knot in the T-shirt to shorten it. I look like a clown in clothes several sizes too big and braced myself for his mockery when I came downstairs.

However, he's not smiling. On the contrary, he doesn't hide the look of desire in his eyes.

Keiron isn't wearing a T-shirt but a low-rise sweatshirt, and I have to say, these Irish guys know how to make a girl happy.

What I said about being hungry? I would easily forgo dinner just to sit and watch them parade their delicious muscles.

"You look fucking gorgeous, girl."

He says suddenly, catching me off guard.

I feel awkward. Even though I've been single for a few years now, I haven't let a guy get close since then. I'm not used to hearing compliments.

Who am I kidding? Even when I was engaged to Simeon, they were rare. The most he did for my self-esteem was say he liked my long, blonde, wavy hair.

"I don't feel beautiful dressed like this."

He lowers the heat on whatever he was cooking and moves closer.

"But do you feel beautiful normally? Because if not, the guys you go out with aren't doing their job right."

"I haven't been out with anyone since Simeon, my ex-fiancé."

"What?"

"I ended my engagement three years ago and haven't been with anyone since."

"Jesus, why not?"

Because after the betrayal I suffered, I don't think I'm capable of trusting a man enough to start a serious relationship. How can I be sure if a guy really wants me or if he's with me for strategic reasons, like Simeon?

Of course, I don't say any of this. I'm not willing to let him or Rourke know how damaged I am.

Nor do I want to remember what I saw that day, as the scene still hurts like a cut from a sharp knife.

"I don't like talking about the past." I step aside, intending to head to the stove. — "I'm starving. I'd rather eat than talk. What's on the menu?"

"Soup. I don't usually cook at home."

I feel the heat of his body against my back, and when I turn, I realize the space between us is minimal, but I don't want to move away.

I lift my head to look at him.

"It smells delicious."

"My mother leaves frozen food once a week."

"Are you still close?" I ask, not out of malice but because I'm pleasantly surprised. It's a good thing he has family nearby. Based on what he told me, I thought he was completely solitary.

"She doesn't blame me," he says, then wraps an arm around my waist and, with the other hand, picks up a remote control from the kitchen island.

He turns it on, and a slow song, which I can't identify, fills the entire apartment.

"I don't like remembering the past either. Now, shake that beautiful ass. You owe me a dance, Russian," he says softly in my ear, as he starts moving our bodies together.

"I never promised you one," I reply, immediately reacting to his touch.

Keiron holds my chin to look at me.

"Haven't you figured out yet that I'm not the type who waits for promises, Tulia? Who cares about them anyway, if we can live for today?"

I dive into the darkness of his eyes, lost in the chocolate-colored iris.

"What are you saying, Keiron? When we arrived, you made it clear you wanted to keep your distance because we were in your territory. This is your sacred space, remember? A place where you don't bring your women."

He pulls me closer, and I feel his hard excitement against my stomach.

My body is on fire, and it has nothing to do with the fact that I haven't had sex in three years, but because the attraction he ignites in me is too intense.

"No, baby" his lips brush lightly against my jaw and slide down my neck "when we got here, I made it clear there's no room for feelings. Lust, however, is always on the table for me."

My heart beats so hard I can feel it against my ribcage.

"I'm not interested in feelings. To fall in love with someone, there needs to be trust, and I will never be able to trust a man again."

"In that case, I think we can come to an agreement..."

He lowers his mouth very close to mine, teasing for a reaction, but at the same time giving me the right to choose.

"This is crazy. We could end up dead."

"No. It will be our secret. When the snow ends, we go back to our lives."

"I..."

He releases me and steps back. Immediately, I miss his body against mine.

"Deny that you want this," he says.

"I've never had casual sex."

He moves closer again, with one hand on each side of the counter, as if trapping me, letting his mouth hover near mine.

"I *only do* casual sex. The dirty, sweaty, hard kind. I'm not into flowers and hearts, but I can make you scream my name while you come so many times that, by the end, it will be the first thing you say when you wake up."

"You're very confident."

"Prove it to me."

"What?"

He bites my lower lip and then licks it. He doesn't do anything more. He stands there, waiting, and I feel my pulse race.

The way he looks at me makes it seem like he's undressing me in his mind. I've never felt so desired by my fiancé as I do by Keiron and Rourke.

I swallow hard and, taking a deep breath to muster courage, wrap my arms around his neck.

It's as if a switch has been flipped because once I crossed that barrier, I don't want to stop.

The sexual tension, which was never far, explodes inside me.

"Kiss me. I don't like to take the initiative. I like..."

"To be controlled during sex?"

"I think so."

"You *think*?"

"Only in bed. Not in any other area of my life, but I fantasize..."

"About what, Tulia?"

My skin is burning as if I were being cooked in a cauldron, but I'm past the stage of embarrassment. I'm on fire for him.

"About domination. Nothing to do with feeling pain. I can't relate sex to pain, but imagining being controlled drives me wild."

A low growl escapes from the back of his throat, and before the next breath, his mouth crashes down on mine.

Keiron's huge hand comes to my neck, and the other lifts me by my ass, hooking a thigh around his hip. When our tongues meet, I feel the pressure in my lower abdomen increase because his kiss is erotic to the point of obscenity.

He mimics, without any subtlety, what I imagine he wants to do to me, and I feel the apex between my thighs dampen.

I slide my hands down his back, scratching lightly, and his grip on my hair tightens.

"I won't make you feel pain. It will all be about pleasure, but you don't need to be gentle with me. If you're going to scratch me, mark my skin, blonde. Forget the good girl act. I want the wild one."

A loud moan escapes me, sensations I've never experienced spreading from my toes to my head.

I feel like lava, incandescent, uncontrollable.

One of his hands slides up under my T-shirt, but before it can reach my breast, I hear a noise, and when I open my eyes, I see Rourke.

Embarrassed, I push Keiron away, who also notices that his friend has arrived and lets go.

"Calm down. No need to be embarrassed, baby. It was just a kiss," he says.

"If that's what you call a kiss, I don't know if I can handle the rest."

He smiles, and the tension in the room lifts.

I don't feel guilty about kissing Keiron. Especially now that I know about Rourke's deceased wife.

He and I are young and free. Rourke is trapped in a memory. I can't compete with her.

"I'll set the dinner plates," I say, more to keep myself busy than to be sure of what I'm actually saying.

I walk past Rourke toward the table and feel his gaze burning into me, but I don't meet his eyes.

I can't handle what the two men stir in me.

Not at the same time.

Chapter 17

Rourke

I hit the punching bag again and again. I'm in the only closed room available, apart from the bedrooms, in Keiron's apartment. It's a small makeshift gym.

I'm not in the habit of working out after dinner, but I feel my body is racing. The energy is flowing from me in endless waves.

For the first time since Viona's death, I'm shaken by a woman.

Desire, I've felt many times. I'm human.

Nothing has made me want to reconsider my vow of celibacy, though.

Until now.

There's something about the Russian blonde that makes my blood pump with a ferocity I've never experienced before.

I don't want to feel this. I don't want to crave pleasure, her skin, her touch.

I don't deserve any kind of reward or joy, and having Tulia, I have no doubt, would be something I'd keep inside me forever.

Before coming downstairs tonight, I made a deal with myself that no matter what happened between her and Keiron, I wasn't going to watch.

Until I saw them kissing.

Until I heard her say she wants to be dominated.

Until I felt my cock swell to the point of pain, imagining her naked on the counter, her pussy devoured by mouths and fingers.

My mouth and fingers, too.

My cock opening her up like a flower.

Looking into her eyes while I take her deeply.

I kick the bag three times in a row, and despite my body starting to show signs of exhaustion, I don't want to go upstairs because I know I won't be able to sleep.

No, that's a fucked-up lie. What I don't want is to catch them again because I know if it happens, I'll stay and watch. I need to see her naked more than I need the next breath.

The door suddenly opens, and they both come in. Keiron in workout shorts, just like me.

"She also wants to throw some punches to try to relax," he says, and I turn my back to them.

"The house is yours," I reply.

"Take off your sweatshirt, baby. You've got my boxer shorts on, right? You need to have your movements free. With the first kick you throw, they'll fall off your body anyway."

I tell myself I won't look, but not even a second passes before I turn back to where she is and watch as she releases the pants that were held up by a fabric belt, probably from the robe.

The garment falls to the floor, and the sight of her in the boxer shorts, which act as a short skirt, her long legs now bare, makes my body react immediately.

Once again, I turn my back to them.

"Have you trained in MMA before?" I ask.

"No." Her voice is very soft. "But I love working out. Anything that wears out the body. I think I've become addicted."

"It's a good alternative to sex," Keiron says, joking, and I hear her laugh.

I don't quite understand what he's talking about.

I use physical exertion to relieve my desire, but with Tulia looking that gorgeous, she must have men all over her like flies to honey. There shouldn't be a lack of opportunities to get laid.

"Do you also compete, like Lorcan?" she asks.

"Not anymore," Keiron replies. "I tore a ligament two years ago. MMA is tough on the body."

"I do," I say.

"Will you teach me?"

I turn to face her, knowing I should say no, but still, I'm certain of what my response will be.

"If you're expecting me to go easy, we might as well not start," I warn.

She lifts her chin.

"Say that after I kick your arrogant ass, Irish."

I shake my head, hiding a smile. I've never met anyone like her. Beautiful, daring, unfiltered, combative, and sexy enough to resurrect the dead.

Half an hour later, we're both sprawled on the floor and Keiron is laughing at us while he massages her feet.

Obviously, I didn't go as hard as I would against an opponent my size, but she's incredibly strong.

Given our physical difference—height and weight—Tulia held out a long time before I beat her.

I have no doubt that if it had been a smaller or less trained man, he'd be leaving here on a stretcher. Her kicks are good, as is the speed with which she moves.

"You could try a career in MMA if everything else goes wrong," I say.

"Are you mocking me?"

"No. I'm serious."

"And why would it go wrong? I'm doing well with the Brotherhood."

Keiron and I look at her with raised eyebrows.

"What's wrong?"

"We know about Leonid's wife, baby," he says.

"I can't talk about it."

"Did you sleep with him or something for his wife to hate you so much?" Keiron asks, indifferent to her protest.

"What? No! Jesus, I told you! I haven't slept with anyone since I broke off the engagement."

Fuck, how is this possible?

As soon as she says it, she covers her face with both arms.

"Great. I think I've embarrassed myself enough. I've just confessed not only that I was betrayed, but that my sex life is non-existent. I'd better go to bed."

Keiron grabs her by the feet, dragging her across the floor until her thighs are on top of his.

Then, he pulls her onto his lap, securing her.

Tulia lets herself stay there, and I can barely breathe, watching everything.

"Get out," a voice yells, but I ignore it.

"Why be embarrassed?" he asks, brushing a strand of her hair away and biting the delicate flesh of her neck.

I feel my mouth water, imagining her taste.

She rolls her eyes, probably because she's naturally insolent, but I can feel her breathing heavier, aware of his caress and his hands on her ass.

"I meant that next to you, I must seem like a nun."

"I like to fuck, but I'm not promiscuous."

"How is that possible?"

"Quality and quantity don't necessarily go hand in hand, darling. The more I get to know a partner's body, the more pleasure we can give each other."

She tries to hide a smile but fails.

"So if we end up snowed in together, will it be an intensive course? Like quantity to reach quality, since we won't have much time together?"

Keiron laughs at the lighthearted joke, and for a second, I feel jealous because she seems to have forgotten I'm here. But then, Tulia turns to me and our eyes lock.

"You never touch, you just watch?" she asks.

"He only watches," Keiron answers for me.

"I touched you in the bedroom," Tulia says, but then, as if feeling embarrassed by what she said, she gets up from Keiron's lap. "Sorry, Rourke. I shouldn't have said that."

My friend looks from one to the other.

"You let her touch you?"

"It wasn't quite like that," Tulia explains, awkwardly. "I'm going to take another shower and then head to bed. Thanks for the workout, Rourke. Goodnight, Keiron."

She bolts before either of us can say a word.

"What was that? Did you change your mind?"

"No," I reply.

I get up as well.

"There's nothing wrong with living a little, Rourke."

"I'm not going to discuss this with you."

I start walking towards the door.

"She feels desire for you too. I don't think Tulia would mind letting you watch."

"She's just a girl in a woman's body, Keiron."

"She's a beautiful woman who hasn't been treated the way she deserves. I'm not looking for love, but when I have her, for however long it lasts, I'll make sure she never doubts herself again. She'll leave knowing just how delicious she is."

I absorb his words and before I leave, I confess:

"She's the only one who's made me want to break the promise I made to never touch another woman in my life."

"What does that mean?"

"Nothing beyond what I said. Have fun."

Chapter 18

Keiron

"**C**an't sleep?" I ask as I find her alone on the first floor. It hasn't been two hours since we all went upstairs, and I heard her footsteps on the stairs.

Tulia doesn't turn immediately.

She's sitting in a nook I have near the full-wall window and seems to be watching the snow fall outside, although I'm sure she can't see much.

The snowstorm has worsened, and according to forecasts, it will be days before it's considered safe to leave the house.

Normally, this would drive me insane. I'm restless, and the idea of being trapped in a concrete prison doesn't make me happy, but the unusual situation, instead of irritating me, excites me. It's as if fate orchestrated this meeting. As if, despite the organizations we're part of, the daily wars, and the internal ones, we were meant to happen.

"I'm lost, Keiron," she finally says as I approach and wrap my arms around her.

I turn her towards me, fitting myself between her legs. The nook provides the perfect height.

"Lost about what, baby?"

"About everything. When Rourke said I should try MMA if nothing else worked out, he had no idea how on point he was."

"I know. Your career has no future with the Organization, no matter if Leonid's wife ever forgives you or not. You'll always carry a stigma."

She nods.

"I don't hold any grudge against her, you know? Sierra was my first mission, and I was doing what I was told," she says vaguely, and I know it's because she can't go beyond what she's revealed, "but I also understand why she'd be upset with me because, in a way, we're similar."

"In what way?"

"Both solitary, hard to trust anyone. I became her friend; that was my role, and then I betrayed her."

"I've done things I'm not proud of in the name of the Syndicate. The difference is that I don't feel remorse. I see it as work. Why did you join the Organization, Tulia? It's clear you have nothing to do with our world."

"First, it was to protect myself."

"What?"

"The person my fiancé cheated on me with didn't want their relationship exposed. My cousin was afraid they'd try to kill me to keep me quiet."

"Fuck me! That ex of yours is also with the Brotherhood! How could you stay around if your life was at risk?"

"I had no choice. I knew nothing beyond the family circle. My cousin is also a soldier with the Organization. She managed to keep me protected."

"The only good thing about this mess is that that son of a bitch is still in Kentucky."

She places her hands on my chest.

"Did you investigate me?" she asks, and only then do I realize I let slip that I knew where she was from without her ever having told me.

"I investigate anyone who comes near me. Don't take it personally."

To my surprise, she shrugs.

"I don't mind. I have nothing to hide except what concerns the Organization."

"Why haven't you gone back to see your family?"

"They don't know the truth and blame me for the end of the relationship. They always thought he was too good for me. Intelligent, handsome, and rich."

"A complete idiot for letting you slip away."

"Have I told you that you do wonders for my ego, Keiron?"

Instead of answering, I trail my tongue along her neck.

"Mmm..."

She hasn't put her sweatshirt back on, so when I pull her by the hips, I feel the perfect outline of her pussy.

It's a light touch, but enough to ignite the fire that's been burning low between us.

I know she can feel how my thick cock presses against the sweatshirt, even under the constraint of my underwear. I don't remember ever reacting with such hunger to a woman.

"Say it again," she requests as I bite the soft flesh of her exposed shoulder.

The T-shirt I lent her is too big and keeps falling off her shoulders.

"Say what, love?"

"Say that there's nothing wrong with me for a man not to desire me."

"You're the most beautiful woman I've ever seen." It's Rourke who answers from behind me, and I pull away slightly to look back.

He's standing near the stairs, watching us.

I hadn't noticed he arrived, but somehow, I knew he would. None of us can resist Tulia.

When I look back at her, her eyes are shining with emotion.

Were his words the cause of that?

Does she not know how beautiful she is?

Yes, the ex-fiancé is indeed a stupid son of a bitch.

Lifting her into my lap and having her wrap her legs around my waist, I sit down on the couch with her straddling me.

Rourke has a perfect view of us from where he's standing, but Tulia is facing away from him. If she has never been with anyone other than her ex-fiancé, I need to guide her slowly to where I want her.

Where — now I'm sure — both of us want, because Rourke can't take his eyes off her.

"Let me show you how beautiful you are, love."

She looks down at her lap, and even in the dim light of the room, I can see how her cheeks are flushed with embarrassment.

"I thought I understood when I said I wanted... when I spoke..."

"That you want to be dominated? Yes, I understood, but you need to know where we're going from here, Tulia. The decision is in your hands, so tell me: do you want him to stay?"

She looks back at Rourke, staring at him for a while. I have no idea what she's thinking, but soon, she nods.

"Yes, I want him to stay, but I need to know something," she says, still facing him. "Do you only watch? I know you don't allow yourself to participate, but can I at least see you too?"

"How do you want to see me, Tulia?" he asks.

She covers her face with both hands.

"I don't know how to say it."

"She wants, when we strip, for you to be naked too, Rourke. Tulia wants to see how excited it makes you to watch her being taken by me. Our girl wants to feel your pleasure."

Chapter 19

Tulia

I can't hide the tremors in my body. I feel bombarded with intense emotions, and so far, all we've exchanged are words.

I want both of them, and it's confusing me.

I don't know how to handle the simultaneous desire for two alpha males. I wasn't raised to be shared between two men but to "belong" to just one, being good, obedient, and not expressing my desires.

I never imagined I would be capable of something like this, but both Keiron and Rourke make me feel secure about myself, and far beyond that, cherished.

I'm not talking about deep feelings, but about a real want.

Raw desire, hunger, need.

God, the looks they give me send shivers of anticipated pleasure through my body.

I remain focused on Rourke after what Keiron says to his friend.

Sitting on his lap, with his calloused hands running over my back, I watch, mesmerized, as my second crush, one of my delicious real-world sexual fantasies, pulls the T-shirt over his head.

I gasp for air, and sensing my anxiety, one of Keiron's hands moves to my hair, gripping with relative force and forcing me to look at him.

"Do you want this?" he asks.

"I've never wanted something so much in my life before," I say honestly.

My body is going through a hormonal and emotional upheaval.

I feel feverish and accelerated, like when we're about to engage in an extreme sport.

The fear of the unknown makes me nervous, but at the same time, I sense that the experience I'm about to have with them will be something I'll remember for the rest of my life.

I barely finish speaking before Keiron's mouth descends upon mine, with a demand completely different from our first kiss.

The tongue demands surrender; its wet heat as it moves between my lips makes the apex between my thighs throb.

The change in his behavior is subtle but unmistakable, and something tells me the game is over.

He's going to give me what I want. He'll dominate me and make me his.

And all of it will be in front of the other man who also drives me wild with desire.

I shiver when his fingers grip the hem of the T-shirt.

Maybe if his movement were abrupt, I would be startled, but contrary to how he gripped my hair and kissed me earlier, he lifts it slowly, leaving me enough space to stop him if I want.

I don't, and when my upper body is exposed, I feel my nipples harden even more from the hungry look Keiron gives me.

I hold back the urge to squirm, while feeling Rourke's eyes burning into my back.

Intuitively, I know he's attentive to every breath I take.

"Turn her to me, Keiron." I hear him command, and my heart races to the point where I can feel it in my ear. "I want to see her too."

See her.

Not us both. He wants *to see me.*

It's silly to focus on this detail. I have no doubt that, given how comfortably they are near each other, they've done this dozens of times.

However, I think he said it on purpose. Rourke is showing me that, despite not touching me due to the promise he made, he desires me.

Keiron turns me around as if I were a doll, now sitting me facing his friend.

He didn't ask me, just did it, and the feeling of not being in control excites me to the point of madness.

I slowly lift my gaze, unable to believe I'm going to face the second man in the room, exposing myself to him without any shame.

Keiron slides his hands along my waist, in a restrained caress, moving closer to my breasts, and Rourke takes a step forward.

He looks from my face to my naked breasts, and I don't know if consciously, he runs his tongue over his lips.

I moan in response. The need vibrating through every cell of my body.

Keiron adjusts me better over his rigid member and now I can feel it from my moist sex to my buttocks as he rubs me back and forth along its length.

I close my eyes as his hands reach my breasts, his fingers initially pulling my nipples gently and then with a hint of pain.

I can't control the moans of pleasure, and he's barely started touching me.

Keiron reaches the edge of the couch, taking me with him, and now my back is against his muscular chest.

I still keep my eyes closed, preferring to stay locked in the sensations.

I hear a movement and, without them saying anything, I know Rourke is kneeling in front of me.

"You said you want to be dominated. It's not because I'm not going to fuck you that I won't tell you what I want from you. Are you ready to obey me, Tulia?"

My heart races and I stare at him as Keiron's hands continue to caress my nipples with more urgency.

I get lost in the intense blue of his eyes for whole seconds before nodding in agreement.

"Speak," he demands.

"I'll obey both of you. I won't say no to whatever you want."

Chapter 20

Rourke

I look at every inch of her like someone thirsty for a rare whiskey.

I want to taste her all over, lick and suck every bit of her milky skin, suck her pink, pointed nipples, hear that beautiful mouth screaming my name.

Keiron's fingers tease her medium-sized breasts, perfect for filling a hand, and even as she looks at me, she can't contain the moans of pleasure he's giving her.

"Stand up and take off your boxer," I say.

I'm close, much closer than I've ever been to any of our partners, and even when Keiron gets her to her feet, I don't move away.

Her lower body is at mouth level. I can smell her arousal.

"Get naked, Tulia," I demand again.

She looks down at me, incredibly beautiful, seeming like a warrior woman.

Strong, yet allowing us to see her vulnerable side, a bit unsure.

Daring and at the same time, soft.

Sweet and spicy.

Tulia is an explosive combination of beauty and sensuality.

She still hesitates, and gasps when Keiron smacks her ass.

"Obey. You are *ours*."

She moans and my cock stirs against the zipper of my jeans.

Without using words, Tulia is showing us how to lead her.

She likes orders. Apparently, she also likes a good smack on the ass.

I watch her hold the waistband of the garment and pull it down slowly.

"Don't look away from me," I command.

The fabric gets tangled around her ankles, but my gaze is fixed on the blonde fuzz, with soft curls, between her thighs.

"Spread your pussy for me. I want to see it."

An intense flush spreads across her face, which drives me even crazier.

She hesitates, and I raise an eyebrow in challenge.

Keiron stands, moving behind her, brushing her ass and pinching a nipple, with his other hand gripping her hip.

"Show him your pretty pussy, baby. Rourke is dying to see how wet you are for both of us."

She gasps and her hands slip down to her legs. Her movements are slow, and I feel my pulse racing at an abnormal pace.

Her long fingers brush the hair before she parts it.

Keiron bites her shoulder, causing her to squeal in surprise.

Tulia finally spreads her thighs, presenting me with the sight of her swollen, slick clitoris.

"I want to suck your pussy. Stick my tongue deep inside. I'm starving for you," I say.

It's not the first time I've given orders during sex, but it's the first time I've expressed my desire so openly. It's also the first time I want to fulfill each one of them without thinking about the consequences.

"Let me touch your face and hair, Rourke. I promise I won't go further. I just want to imagine..."

"What?" Keiron asks. "Do you want to imagine he's sucking you, naughty girl? Or both of us at the same time? A mouth on your pussy, eating you hard, and the other sucking your tits?"

She closes her eyes for a second and we have the answer we need.

I take her hands and bring them to my face. She slides one through my hair, gripping it firmly, and even this small action excites me immensely.

At the same time, Keiron parts her lips and finger fucks her clit.

Tulia writhes, moans, and her grip on my hair becomes urgent.

"Yes, I want to fantasize about both of you on me," she confesses, and it seems to break the last bit of control Keiron has.

"I need to taste her," he says.

I rise as well, and now she is caught between us. I don't touch her with my hands, but my bare chest brushes against her delicious breasts.

"Hold her while I suck her," he asks me. "You won't be doing anything else, but I want you to open her up for me, offer her to my mouth."

I don't take my eyes off hers, the refusal, born of guilt, on the tip of my tongue, though desire is quickly gaining ground.

"Is this what you want, Tulia?"

The flush deepens, but she doesn't back down.

"I want to be in your arms, even if you don't do anything to me," she says. "I need both of your hands on me. I've been dreaming about this since that first night at the bar."

I lower my face to the curve of her neck to smell her.

Accepting what she's asking is like playing with fire, but I convince myself that I'll do nothing but keep her close to me.

I take a step back and pull down my jeans, leaving the boxer. The steel-hard erection makes the head of my cock push over the waistband of the underwear.

Keiron hands her to me, turning her around and making her ass come towards me.

I wrap an arm around her waist, restricting her movements, and whisper in her ear:

"Not like this."

Before she has a chance to take another breath, I lift her onto my lap and sit on the sofa with her on top of me.

I moan as I feel her ass cheeks part to accommodate my hard cock.

Her hands move to my face and hair, the tips of her fingers gentle in an innocent caress, but my arousal has reached a point where just looking at her makes my shaft throb.

I hold her thighs over my forearms, spreading her as far as she'll go, and I would give anything to see her now.

"Look at me. While he's eating your pussy, it's me you'll see, Tulia."

At the first touch of Keiron's tongue, she screams and writhes on my cock; I almost go insane seeing the raw desire on her face.

"You're delicious, Russian," he says. "And all ours."

"Is this what you want, my blonde?" I ask. "To have two men at your feet, fulfilling your desires?"

"*You* two. No others would do," she moans, lifting her hips as he intensifies the sucking.

My hands tighten on her thighs, and deep down, in the unconscious, a voice whispers that this isn't just a "holding," but I silence it because if I don't have at least a small piece of her skin on me, I'll go mad.

I don't know what she sees on my face while I look at her; maybe a primitive hunger, because suddenly, her writhing on my lap doesn't seem like a result of losing control over her pussy being devoured. It's a rhythmic, uninterrupted motion, like showing me how it would be if I were between her thighs, inside her.

One hand goes to a breast and pulls the nipple, while the other holds Keiron's head where it needs to be.

Tulia, like both of us, is starving. Her unabashed desire, the courage to surrender when I know this isn't her nature, is even more exciting than if she were experienced.

Fucking her with one and then two fingers, Keiron rises and sucks her breasts, alternating between them, but it doesn't seem enough, so he grabs both together.

I've seen him in action many times. Like me, he enjoys sex, but he's never seemed so out of control.

A previously unknown feeling in our joint play brings an incredibly strange sensation to my chest.

I can't identify what it is until she moans unmistakably, showing me that she's very close to orgasm.

Jealousy.

I want to be the one to make her come first.

I've never experienced such a strong conflict in my life and the grip of my fingers on her thighs tightens, becoming almost cruel.

It seems to drive her even crazier and I don't think she knows what she's saying when, writhing on my lap, she asks:

"Kiss me, Rourke. I want to come while kissing you."

Before I even open my mouth to respond, I know I'm going to give her what she wants.

Desire flows from me in powerful, violent waves.

I spread her thighs even further.

"Suck her pussy. Make her come on your face, Keiron."

As I give that order, I bring her hands back to my neck, taking control of the touches on her breasts, and with the other, I pull her mouth to mine.

He has his face between Tulia's thighs, but I'm the one dominating every piece of her desire.

I feast on her mouth in a voracious attack and without questioning my decision, Keiron devours her as well.

Her body arches as my friend continues to enjoy his feast; I'm dying to know what flavor she has.

He holds our girl's ass cheeks and brings her sex to his face, his mouth coating with her honey.

Alternates between sucking and fucking her drenched opening with his fingers.

I reach my limit.

I move his hand away from her swollen clit, replacing it with my thumb. At the first touch on the sensitive flesh, Tulia explodes into an endless orgasm, her body trembling as it writhes over me.

"Fuck, you're so tasty!" he roars.

Adrenaline sets every cell in my body on fire; Tulia's excitement, her pleasure, erasing any doubt about what I want.

"I'm going to fuck you so hard," I promise.

She's still looking at me, although she seems limp in my arms.

"Do it. I don't care. I want everything with you. Teach me."

Chapter 21

Keiron

I f it were any other guy, I'd have told him to back off. I don't mind being seen fucking. There's not a drop of shyness running through my veins, but I've never shared a woman.

And Tulia? Well, she's not just any girl, she's a delight. The kind I don't want anyone else near while she's mine because I know that when I have her for the first time, I'm not stopping anytime soon.

But this is Rourke. Not just a comrade-in-arms, but almost a brother.

I've seen all the hell he's been through in the past few years. The guilt that almost drove him to follow Viona to the grave.

Before Tulia came into our lives, he never showed any real interest in a woman.

Desire, yes, but nothing that would make him backtrack on his vow of celibacy.

And I know it's mutual. Despite being crazy about her and feeling jealous of my Russian, I've seen how much Tulia is into him too. She wants both of us.

"Come here, pretty girl. You deserve more than a cramped sofa."

I pull her off Rourke's lap, and now that she's coming down from her orgasm, she looks a little shy.

I can still taste her honey on my tongue. The woman has an addictive flavor.

I don't look back as I climb the stairs, but I know Rourke is following me.

The decision he made to participate actively today surprised the hell out of me. He must be as thirsty to taste her as I am.

Her body trembles as I walk.

"Nervous?"

"Yes. I'm not the most self-confident person in the world. I don't know what to do."

"There's no script, beautiful. Just pleasure. Surrender, and we'll take care of the rest."

I set her down on the floor and for a few seconds, I admire her beautiful body.

I look at her to make sure she's with us, sure of what she wants, and I see her eyes moving from me to him, as if she can't decide.

Rourke stops beside me, but it seems that now that he's decided to claim her, something has broken inside him, and he's not willing to wait.

He goes to her and, grabbing her neck, pulls her in for a kiss. I never thought I'd get turned on watching another guy touching the woman I want, but seeing the rough way he takes her, watching Tulia surrender into his hands, makes my cock harden even more.

I position myself behind her. I pull her hair to the side and nip at her earlobe.

Tulia moans into Rourke's mouth, pressing her ass against my cock.

I slide my hand between their bodies and stroke her clit.

She whimpers, writhing even more against me.

"You're right. She's so tasty, Keiron, but I need to taste her for myself."

He kneels in front of her and, moving my hands away from her pussy, puts one of Tulia's thighs over his shoulders.

Tulia throws her head back, completely surrendered to his tongue, mouth, and teeth.

I undress and, spreading her ass cheeks, rub my cock between them. She stiffens, tensing.

"Shhhh... I'm just feeling you. Everything we do will be with your consent, love. Relax and enjoy. Anything that makes you uncomfortable, just say. Whatever happens between us will always be pleasure, baby, just a 'stop' and we'll listen. But other than that, you obey like a good girl."

She surrenders again into our arms, and I swear to myself that I won't abuse her trust.

I pinch her nipples, starting a back-and-forth motion with my cock between the cheeks of her ass, and the combination with Rourke's sensations eating her pussy breaks her control completely.

Tulia is on tiptoes, trying to make the most of both of us, and very quickly, my desire reaches a dizzying level.

"Let's take her to bed. I want that mouth on me," I say.

"Not yet. She's going to give me a drink first."

I lift her by the legs, placing both thighs over his shoulders, pushing her towards Rourke's tongue.

"Oh my God..." she moans as Rourke penetrates her with his tongue.

"So beautiful and ours. Do you like not having control over your own body, Russian?"

She nods, and I see his thumb working in circular motions on her nerves, while he fucks her with three fingers now.

"Your pussy is beautiful, just like you, but it's very tight too. I need to prepare you," he says, and the words seem to make her even more aroused, because she takes one of my hands and brings it to her mouth, nibbling and licking the tips of my fingers.

He pushes his fingers inside her rhythmically, and every time he enters her sex, Tulia writhes in my arms.

Rourke sucks on her clit, his face buried in her blonde pubes, but when she starts showing signs that she's about to come, he seems to change his mind.

He rises, and Tulia's protest at not getting her prize is fucking sexy. All female, wanting to be satisfied.

"Calm down, my delight. You'll get everything you want."

Rourke takes her from my arms and leads her to the bed. He positions her so that her head hangs off the edge of the mattress; with that, I already know what he has in mind.

Like me, he's noticed that Tulia wants the full experience. She wants to be fucked by both of us at the same time.

He kneels between her thighs, and our blonde needs to lift her head, which was unsupported, to look at him.

"I'm going to make you come while you suck his cock," he says. "We're clean. I haven't fucked in years. I said you haven't either, so I assume you're protected. Keiron never fucks without a condom, but it's up to you how we'll do this."

He sounds almost clinical, and despite the conversation being somewhat of a mood killer, it's very necessary.

Her cheeks flush even more before she finds the courage to respond:

"If we're clean, I... uh... prefer to taste him without anything."

"Suck me," I say.

"What?"

"Lie down," I order, holding her by the shoulders and making her lower her head again. "You're not going to prove anything to me, baby. You're no longer the nice bride of that asshole who didn't know how to value you. With us, you can let go. Let us see you as you really are, Tulia. You're not going to prove anything. You're going to *suck* my delicious cock and make me come down your throat."

Before her face can flush any redder, I kneel and give her a wet kiss, thrusting my tongue into her delicious mouth, while Rourke goes back to working on her pussy.

As much as I want those plump lips around my cock, I can't stop kissing her. Tulia is all soft, her tongue included. She's receptive and sweet.

The girl moans loudly at something Rourke does and writhes her hips like a cat in heat.

I stand up and masturbate, watching her generous lips part in a long whimper. Tulia is dying with desire and eager to come.

I hold her shoulders to position her better, and this time, they both protest.

I smile.

"Come here, my beauty."

Her head is hanging completely now, and I lean in, brushing my cock against her lips and pressing her two breasts together. I fit myself in there, my balls hitting her chin while I fuck her tits.

"Open your mouth for me, Tulia."

She obeys and doesn't take her lust-filled eyes off mine. However, she can't keep still. She writhes on Rourke's face, who gives her no respite. He must be starving after so many years without sex.

"Suck," I command, holding her face with both hands. "I just want your mouth on me. Use your hands to pull on those hard nipples."

She starts caressing her breasts but hesitates before she begins to suck me. Her tongue slips out and lightly circles the head. It's delightful, but not what I want.

"Suck my cock, beautiful. I want to see if you can take it all the way down your throat."

I force my erection into her mouth, pushing slowly, making her take more and more of me.

"Relax your jaw, my love. I'm not going to hurt you."

She does as instructed, and when I feel not just sliding but being sucked by her warm mouth, I moan in pleasure.

Once she gets the hang of it, she sucks eagerly, and I know I won't last long this first time.

As if attuned to both of us, Rourke increases his pace in fucking her, and Tulia explodes in his mouth, without any modesty.

"Don't come yet," he says. "I want to fuck her while she sucks you."

Chapter 22

Rourke

Before putting her on all fours as I want, I bring her to me, positioning her on her knees on the bed so we can look at each other. I want Tulia to be sure that, in what's happening between us, she also has control.

"Is everything still okay, baby?"

She nods and then licks her lips.

"I want more."

Jesus Christ!

Few guys would be able to see a goddess like her begging to be fucked and keep their sanity, but I'm not rushing anything.

"Let's see what I can do for you."

I spin her around and put her on her hands, with her knees on the bed. Without wasting time, Keiron slots himself between her lips, thrusting deeply into the mouth of our Russian.

Surprised, she pushes her tight ass back, begging for my cock.

I bite both cheeks and spread them wide, tasting her at the opening where, now I know, she is still a virgin.

Just as when Keiron started masturbating in her ass, she tenses up.

I don't stop. Tulia knows she has the power to say no, so I understand that she's not refusing, just doesn't know what kind of pleasure this is.

"Ah, fuck, girl. Your mouth is paradise," Keiron moans, stroking her hair.

I hold her by the hips, my fingers digging into her white flesh, the tension from controlled desire spreading painfully through my body.

"Last chance to ask me for a condom, love," I warn.

She stops what she's doing and looks back. Slowly, she shakes her head, signaling no.

"I want to feel you, Rourke."

My hands travel down her back. I slide a finger along her spine.

I grip her hips, closing my eyes for a moment and trying to find the guilt I always carry inside me, but the only thing holding me back right now is my ravenous hunger for her.

Keiron holds her face, and I grab her from behind. Tulia is entirely in our hands.

"Just like that. Open your little mouth wide for me," he asks, and I reach my limit.

I brush the tip of my cock against her wet entrance and lean forward, biting her back.

She squirms against me, and I know she's eager too.

I slot myself into her soaked sex and almost groan with pleasure when I feel skin against skin.

I caress her hair before securing my hand in it, wrapping it around my fist.

I push, trying to go as slowly as I can, even though it feels like it might give me a stroke, but Tulia, as I had already noticed when I made her come on my fingers, is very tight.

I force myself between the folds, sliding the head of my cock, and she moans in a mix of protest and arousal.

"Fuck! Keep doing whatever you're doing, Rourke," Keiron pleads.

Her scent is taking over the room, driving me even crazier, and when I see her beautiful ass slip out of my control, I stop her, restricting her movements and sliding into her pussy in a long stroke.

Damn!

Even though she doesn't ask me to stop, she throws her body forward, making Keiron enter her mouth even deeper.

He grunts, not hiding his pleasure.

I keep her trapped where I want, and unable to wait any longer, I pull out and shove everything back in.

Shit, if I don't focus, I'm going to come much faster than I anticipated. She's so damn good.

I pull out of her heat and rub the swollen head of my cock against her clit.

Without stopping sucking Keiron, she moans a "please" that robs me of what's left of my sanity.

I push back in fully and stop at the depths of her body, letting her feel me, teaching her how I like to be received.

"Stay on your heels, Keiron. I want her ass in the air."

He does as I ask, and the sight of Tulia naked, completely exposed to me, pleasuring him with her mouth, is a scene I will never forget.

I stand up and lower my body, slotting back into her, my hands on her hips.

I thrust deeply inside her and hold myself there. We both moan because in this position, she grips me like a vice.

I start moving, hammering into her delicious pussy, and each time, my balls smack against her hard clit.

One of my hands holds her like a claw while the other dives into the juncture between her thighs, massaging her bundle of nerves.

"I hope you're ready, love."

With that last warning, I start to fuck her hard, forcing myself relentlessly inside her sex.

At no point, despite knowing I'm big for her, does Tulia try to escape my control, which drives me even more wild.

For a long time, I pump inside her, completely lost in the world around me, vaguely hearing the moans of all three of us.

She tightens around my cock, and I know she's close to climax.

I increase the speed, and she gasps, her body tense with desire in my hands.

I hold her shoulders like a lever, and eagerly, she pushes hard against me.

I give her ass a hard smack.

"Don't do that. I'll give you everything you want, but I don't want to hurt you."

"Oh, fuck!" Keiron grunts as she sucks him deeper.

Tulia lets out a moan of pleasure, completely filled by both of us.

Her entire body trembles from the demand of our possession, her skin goosebumps with arousal.

I force every inch of my cock into her pussy, and the tight opening resists my thrust, making the intrusion even more delicious.

I move faster, and now her face is fully buried in Keiron's lap.

"I'm going to come," he warns, standing up. "Lift her. I want my cum on those tits."

I change positions, sitting back on my heels as he was moments ago, and pull her onto my lap.

She sinks down tightly, almost to the point of pain, and when she tries to lift off, I don't let her.

"You're not going anywhere. I want you taking all of me, sitting and grinding. Obey me."

She turns her face back, and for a moment, I need to look away from her eyes because the trust she shows in me stirs emotions I don't want to feel.

I wrap my arms around her waist, and soon enough, the spell turns against the spellcaster, the sensation of being fully buried makes me dizzy with desire.

Keiron jerks off in front of her face.

"Have you already swallowed?" he asks.

She shakes her head.

"I'm going to give you a taste, baby. Hold her jaw, Rourke."

I caress her jaw before firmly holding it.

"Stick out your tongue, my lovely. I'm going to feed you."

I touch the center of her wet folds while thrusting my cock inside her.

Obediently, she grinds as I instructed, allowing for even more delicious penetration.

Her head rests against my chest, giving me a perfect view of what's about to happen.

Keiron's hand works faster and the instant the first spurt of semen hits her tongue, she comes too, convulsing in my arms.

Tulia licks her lips, collecting what escaped, and he strokes her cheek, smiling.

He leans down and kisses her mouth before moving away to the bathroom.

I spin her off my body and lay her on the bed, bringing her legs across my shoulders.

Without gentleness, I thrust into her pussy up to the base.

She moans loudly, taking me in.

Every time I pull out and push back in, I clench my jaw because she's so tight.

I pound into her without rest, and her wet walls restrict me.

"Please."

I'm on the edge of coming, my cock sliding in and out of her with increasing urgency.

The friction of our skin, my hard flesh forcing against her softness, Tulia's eyes on mine... The whole scene contributes to a kind of liquid fire spreading through my veins.

I don't want the connection. I just need the pleasure she can give me, so I force myself to stay aware that it's just sex.

I run a finger through her folds, stimulating her clitoris, and as if she can't handle the sensations, she closes her eyes.

I want her eyes on me.

I'm aware that I'm a fucking contradiction right now, so I choose to deal only with the attraction.

I lift her off the bed and sit, making her mount me facing forward, diving into her wet pussy. Tulia envelops me in her warmth, keeping me captive to her sex with constant contractions.

I grab her ass, making her almost bounce on my lap, fucking her wildly.

It's a brutal contrast to what we were doing moments ago, but she seems to embrace my madness, our desire meeting halfway.

With increasing intensity, I make her sit on me. Her ass hitting my thighs, my cock pounding and thrusting into her mercilessly.

"I want to fill you up," I say.

Her pupils dilate and her arms wrap around my neck.

"Take all of me, Rourke. I'm on the pill and I want everything from you."

The unexpected confession pushes me to the limit.

"Delicious."

I lower my mouth and capture a nipple, not diminishing the ferocity with which I fuck her.

I see her put her hand between us, fingering her clitoris, desperate to come, and with each touch, she moans even more surrendered and filthy.

I grip the cheeks of her ass tightly, thrusting in and out of her five, six times before commanding:

"Come, Tulia. I need to see your face while you come for me."

As she screams her surrender, soaking me with her orgasm, my hands spread her buttocks, making her even more exposed.

My movements become urgent, the speed with which I pump into her is animalistic.

"Come on me," she begs, and that's my trigger.

I push one last time before spilling everything inside her.

Chapter 23

Tulia

I wake up feeling like my body has been beaten. I have an athletic build and with the amount of physical exercise I do, getting myself tired is no easy feat, but I feel as if I've spent forty-eight hours at the gym without a break.

At first, I'm disoriented about where I am. The room is dark and I can't remember if I slept for a few minutes or for days.

And then, slowly, memories start to come back.

Jesus, I did that!

Keiron and Rourke. I was with both of them at the same time.

I sit up in bed, trying to get my bearings, afraid of tripping and waking them, because now I kind of understand that this isn't the room I was staying in.

And then, I feel him.

Before he even stretches out his arm to turn on the light, I feel his eyes on me in the dim room.

When the room lights up, I see Rourke sitting in the armchair, about three meters away, even more handsome than I remember.

No, it hasn't been hours. Just a few minutes since we both came. The moisture between my thighs confirms this.

He doesn't move, his muscular arms resting on his bare legs. He's wearing only a pair of boxers.

He says nothing, just keeps looking at me.

I don't know what it is about the Irishman that affects me so much. Maybe it's the fact that I see in his solitude a reflection of my own. The thing is, every time we lock eyes, I get lost in those beautiful eyes, feeling like I've known him for a long time.

And then, a door opens and the spell is broken.

Keiron is back. His body still dripping from the shower and only a black towel wrapped around his waist.

At the moment, I'm the center of attention for both of them and I should be dying of embarrassment for being naked, but instead, the desire I see in their eyes makes me feel powerful.

"I've prepared a bath for you. I just had one myself, but if you want company..." Keiron says, leaving the rest unsaid.

I stand up, not bothering to cover myself with the sheet. They've both already seen me in the most intimate way possible.

"No," I reply, perhaps a bit too quickly. "I mean, I think I'd prefer to do this alone."

As soon as I finish speaking, I know I've made a mistake.

Both of them come closer, showing concern.

Keiron, with that model-like face from a towel commercial, and Rourke, completely at ease with his own body, like a tattooed Adonis.

He's the first to approach and, holding my chin, forces me to look at him.

"Are you okay?"

I force a smile, even though I'm feeling very embarrassed now.

"I'm fine."

"Are you sure?" Keiron asks.

"Yes. I'm going to enjoy my bath and then we could eat... What do you think?"

Keiron nods, heading towards the door.

"We'll meet you in the kitchen," Rourke says, though his tone still shows concern.

Keiron, however, as always, lightens the serious mood.

"Come down naked, love. I have plans for you and a can of whipped cream."

I almost run out after he says that, but I can still hear his laughter before he closes the bathroom door.

Great! If they had any lingering doubts about me being a country girl, they'd be gone right now.

After everything that happened, feeling shy right now, Miss Tulia?

I step into the water, sitting in the large bathtub and stretching out my legs. I almost moan with pleasure as the soothing warmth envelops me.

My muscles are sore, but I can hardly wait for the whipped cream fun.

I had more orgasms tonight than during my entire time dating and engaged.

Thinking about Simeon makes my stomach churn. I don't want to bring him into our haven, not even through memories.

I know what happened will last as long as the snowstorm and then can't be repeated, but while we're here, they're both mine.

Sir!

Both of them!

Sir, who would have thought! From a naive girl to a woman with the courage to go for a ménage.

I squirt a bit of liquid soap on the sponge and for several minutes I'm completely absorbed in taking care of myself, my body deliciously satisfied.

Now and then, a sneaky thought crosses my mind about what it would be like, in a real world, to have one of them as a boyfriend, but I push the idea away.

Thinking about something like that will only create expectations that will never be fulfilled, which will hurt me.

ALMOST HALF AN HOUR later, I return to my room with a towel wrapped around me.

As tempting as it is to forget everything else and pretend my life revolves around having sex with two gods of lust, I have a duty to the Organization.

I grab my phone and call Taisiya.

She answers only on the sixth ring, and my intuition tells me she was doing the same thing I was a few minutes ago.

"Hi, Tulia. I'm fine. Is there nothing else to do?" she says, like a machine gun.

I roll my eyes.

"Actually, there is. But since I've been given the thankless task of taking care of a nun, I needed to check on you. Sierra hating me is bad enough. I don't need to incur Anastacia's wrath as well."

"My sister would never hate you. I'll tell her we're best friends."

"And why would you do that?"

"I kind of like your sassy attitude."

I smile.

Taisiya, if she goes through with the "career," which I very much doubt, will be the craziest nun ever.

"I don't want to meddle in your life. You're an adult, but I'll ask you to be careful. Whatever you do there could have consequences."

"I'd say the same to you."

I feel my face heat up.

"I don't understand."

"You do understand, but I'm not indiscreet and I'm also very good at keeping secrets."

After that, she hangs up.

God, was I so obvious that others noticed my interest in Keiron and Rourke?

How embarrassing!

I do my best to keep the blood from rushing to my face, but there's no help for it. I feel heat warming my cheeks.

I know I'm free, just like they are. We didn't do anything wrong—except for being from rival organizations—but still, a threesome goes against how I was raised.

It's a taboo even for regular people who consider themselves liberal. For my family? It would be like buying a one-way ticket to hell.

I feel a bitter smile pulling at my mouth as I remember what made me run away that day, which in my memory feels as distant as if it happened in another life.

"Don't think about it," a voice advises. *"Damn the judgment of others. Damn the hypocrisy you were raised with."*

Determined to get everything I can out of this impromptu vacation, I let the towel fall to the floor and head to the kitchen completely naked, just as Keiron instructed.

Chapter 24

Keiron

"How's your head after what happened?"

He shrugs.

"It's just sex."

"I didn't say it wasn't."

"I don't want to talk about it. During the time we're here, I'm going to indulge in forgetting the past."

"God knows I needed that. It's just..."

"What?"

"I don't know how to say this without sounding ridiculous," I say, filling a mug with coffee for each of us and handing him one. "I'm a lone wolf. I've never been and don't plan to be in a serious relationship, but you and Tulia... man, you were married and the girl, as far as we know, was on the doorstep of the church when she decided to leave her whole life behind."

"What does that mean?"

"I don't know, damn it, but it seems like neither of you have the profile of someone who hooks up casually."

"I can speak for myself, not for her. I've found love in this life. Regardless of us being from rival organizations, and even now that I've broken my celibacy, I'm not looking for commitment. I don't want a girlfriend."

Neither of us noticed Tulia approaching.

And only when I look over his shoulder does Rourke realize we're no longer alone.

For a fraction of a second, I see a trace of disappointment on Tulia's face after what he said. I wasn't wrong. There's something more between them. A connection that I've never managed or even wished to have with anyone.

In the blink of an eye, however, her expression changes to one of defiance, and she starts walking toward me as if on a mission.

I've seen many angry women.

Who am I kidding? I've done a good job along my way to annoy a few, especially with my... let's say... *instability* in relationships.

She currently seems to have a target to destroy, and that target is him.

I almost smile at the thought until I see her in full and realize she did as I told and came to us completely naked.

"Am I dressed correctly for our meeting?" she asks provocatively, doing a full three hundred sixty degrees turn.

I feel like my tongue is glued to the roof of my mouth, desire hitting me like the gallop of a wild horse.

I don't even remember what I was talking about, or that we're not alone. I can't focus on anything but her.

"Come here, gorgeous," I call, extending my hand.

I don't know if she's pretending not to see him because she heard what he said or if right now she only wants me. To be honest, I don't care. I don't mind being used as a way for her to vent her anger at Rourke. I need to have her again.

I lift her up and sit her on the kitchen counter.

"I thought I mentioned something about games and whipped cream, so I'll give you a hint: I love sweets."

She smiles and gives me a sexy wink.

Jesus, the woman is an erotic dream in the flesh. She looks like a confident goddess, certain her worshippers will do anything to possess her. As far as I'm concerned, she's absolutely right.

"Lie down and plant your feet on the marble," I command, and for a second or two, our eyes meet and her confidence seems to leave her, but then she obeys.

I've never been one for fetishes. I like to fuck, but I don't have fantasies that need to be fed when the sex is over, but I swear I'd love to be able to film her like this: sprawled on my kitchen counter, waiting to be devoured.

I go to the fridge and grab the can of whipped cream. Taking my time, I return to her and place it on the counter.

"Spread your thighs for me."

Now I can feel Rourke's tension, his heavy breathing, and I'm almost certain I know what it is: jealousy.

However, he just declared that what we have here is casual, so I'm not going to stop fucking her while there's a damn snowflake falling from the sky.

"How far are you willing to go in our games?"

"My only limit is something that causes me unbearable pain."

"Slaps on the ass?"

Her cheeks turn red.

"I have no problem with that."

I pull her closer to the edge of the counter, leaving the lower part of her body almost in the air, but her feet keep her from falling.

I take the can of whipped cream and spread a generous amount over her sex and between the cheeks of her ass.

I don't mention where we're going from here. She's an intelligent girl, and I know she's received a clear hint that I plan to push her limits a bit now.

I run a finger through the cold topping and bring it to her lips.

"Suck."

She parts her lips, allowing me to advance. She sucks slowly, and my cock, already hard, turns to steel.

I bury my face in her pussy, licking all the cream, and when I reach her clit, she moans with pleasure.

Out of the corner of my eye, I see Rourke moving closer. To my surprise, she says:

"No. This time, you're just going to watch. Isn't that what you've always liked to do? I'm no different from the others, right? Let's see how well you can keep your self-control."

There's a silent exchange between the two of them, and for a moment, he says nothing.

What Tulia might not realize is that Rourke is as alpha as I am.

"Let's put her on the coffee table," he says.

I lift her up, and by the time we reach the living room, he has cleared the coffee table of any objects.

I lay her down and position her legs the same way they were on the counter. I bend down and lick the rest of the whipped cream, this time extending the licks to her ass.

I caress the untouched area, playing with my tongue and the tip of my finger. She tenses around me but moans with pleasure.

Rourke approaches.

"Did I say I like to watch?" he asks. "You're right. But do you know what else I do?"

"Besides lusting after me?" Tulia provokes.

He ignores her comment.

"I give orders, and you'll obey each one. The only times I'll touch you will be to position you better for Keiron. If you want my cock and mouth on you, you'll have to ask for it."

I notice that his words excite her, and Tulia's reaction increases my arousal as well.

However, I'm not going to fuel the damn war between them. We're here to have fun.

I give her ass a playful smack.

"Back to our conversation, my blonde: you said your only limit is pain. How much pain?"

She answers me, but looking at Rourke:

"Something that makes me beg you to stop. That will be my limit."

"I want to fuck your ass," I say.

Certainly, I'd never win the label of Prince Charming, but I've never pretended to be one.

"I don't..."

"I know you don't, but something tells me you want the full experience. We can take it slow, trying each thing. You'll decide what's pleasurable or not."

She bites her lower lip, thoughtful. Then, she looks towards the window, and I guess she's considering how long the snowstorm will last.

Not much, if the message I received about an hour ago on my phone is correct. Maybe another day.

"He already said he won't hurt you, and if by chance something happens, a word from you and it's over. Are you afraid?"

Rourke's words come out as a challenge, and you can see the provocation behind them. He expects her to back down. In fact, my guess is that he wants her to back down.

We both know that, no matter that she's twenty-three, Tulia is very inexperienced with sex.

There's something more, however, that maybe only I've noticed: Rourke is becoming possessive over her and wants Tulia to say *"back off."*

Even lying on the table, in a position that some would consider vulnerable, she lifts her chin to face him. Then she shakes her head in a negative gesture.

"What does that mean?" she asks. "No, I want to continue," or "no, I don't feel ready"?

"Yes, I want to try everything," she says, and for a moment, I have the feeling that he's going to go back on his word and grab her by the hair for a kiss, but instead, he just stares at me and says:

"Get condoms and lubricant."

Chapter 25

Tulia

"You don't need to prove anything to any of us," he says as Keiron leaves the room, probably to get what was requested.

I count to ten in my head before responding. I don't even know why I'm feeling so crazy.

Liar. You know why.

I heard him talking about what happened between the three of us and it upset me.

I know what we have is experimental sex and that in the long run, anything more lasting would be impossible, but Rourke broke years of celibacy to be *with me*, and that has to mean something.

I'm feeling insecure, and I never react well when I'm rejected.

No, he didn't reject me. He compared me to his deceased wife by saying that he's already found a love in his life, and that hit all my fears of never being good enough for a man.

"Maybe I don't want to prove something to you, but to myself," I say, feigning confidence and sliding my hands over my breasts. I stop at my nipples, which are already hard, and pull on both.

I see his gaze following the movement and I want to squeeze my stomach.

I'm still sprawled out like a wanton on the table, with Rourke standing at my side. He's wearing low-rise sweatpants that do nothing to hide his erection, though he doesn't seem worried about it.

"What, for example?"

"Huh?"

"You said maybe you want to prove something to yourself. What is it, Tulia?"

I spread my thighs and his gaze drops to my sex.

"My wild side." I spread my legs a little more. "I never thought about anal sex until I met you guys."

He looks dangerous, like he might pounce on me at any moment.

I want it more than my next breath.

"Touch yourself, Tulia. I can smell you from here and it's driving me crazy."

To provoke him, I slide a finger over my clit.

I'm trembling. I've never seen myself as a sensual woman, but Rourke and Keiron make me feel like a sex goddess.

I've masturbated before, of course, but the fact that he's watching makes the intensity of the sensation triple, and I moan before I can hold back.

"Never thought about anal sex?"

"No, but now I'm curious."

"Just ask, sweetheart. I'm at your disposal."

He's tempting me because he wants me to give in and beg. We both know the desire is mutual.

"In your dreams, Irishman. You'll have to ask if you want to be my first. I don't think Keiron would mind."

For the love of all that's holy, someone shut me up.

I don't know which entity possessed me to challenge him this way, but I want it to leave my body now because from the look Rourke is giving me, I'm in deep trouble.

"I don't have a fixation on virgins in any sense, buddy," Keiron says, coming back into the room.

I need to break this invisible bond my foolish heart is trying to forge. I have to remind myself of what Rourke said earlier, in the kitchen.

The memory is enough to bring my irritation back.

Does he think he's immune to me? I'm more than willing to test that.

I kneel on the table and curl my index finger in a *come here* gesture to Keiron, completely ignoring Rourke.

I've never done anything even remotely like this, but I need to prove to him—and to myself—that I'm the queen of casual sex.

Keiron, as cheeky as ever, removes the only piece of clothing he had on, his boxer briefs, and stops with his rock-hard erection right in front of my face. He moves his hand as if to grab me by the hair, but to my astonishment, Rourke intervenes:

"No. I'll control her for you," Rourke says.

Without me anticipating what he's going to do, Rourke grabs my hair in his fist and pushes my head toward Keiron's sex.

A mix of sensations so intense happens inside me that I can't identify which is the strongest.

Rourke's big hand in my hair, guiding me to Keiron, makes the moisture between my thighs increase, but it's the contact with both of their bodies at the same time that drives me to the brink of madness.

I test my tongue slowly on his sex, glancing from one to the other. Neither of them blinks, focused on my movements.

"Open your mouth wide, Tulia," Keiron commands, with a hoarse voice.

I obey, and he slides all the way in, without gentleness, while Rourke holds my head steady.

I close my eyes and savor his taste, but I'm trembling also from Rourke's grip on my hair.

I feel fingers caressing my cheek, and when I open my eyes, Keiron is watching me take him with a tense expression.

"You're fucking perfect, Russian."

I see Rourke use his free hand to remove his sweatshirt, and his erect member springs proudly and thickly a few inches from me.

My pulse races as he starts to masturbate. His eyes focused while I pleasure his friend.

Keiron moves in and out of me, establishing a rhythm, but after a while, he lowers and lifts me, taking us to the sofa.

"Just pleasure, my blonde. If you stay kneeling on the table, it will be more painful than necessary."

I have the feeling it wasn't just for that reason he moved me from the table. I caught a look between the two of them, a kind of silent communication.

As I suspected, he doesn't position me as I was before. He lies down, sitting me astride his thighs.

For a moment, I don't know where Rourke is until he appears at my side and, holding my face with both hands, brushes his thick member against my lips and orders:

"Suck."

I'm sure I'm going to faint. It can't be healthy, the pace my heart is beating right now.

"Why can't you resist me?" I ask, trying to buy time and calm myself down.

He doesn't smile as he says:

"Yes, because I can't resist you." He uses his thumb to caress my lips. "I'm going to come in your mouth and then, fuck your virgin ass."

If any other man said something like that, I'd tear out his tongue. But being him, to my shame, I shiver in response. My whole body tingling with desire.

Chapter 26

Rourke

Her eyes shine with raw passion, and without me asking, she parts her lips to let me in.

Keiron sits down to lick her breasts, taking turns between the two of us, and every moan of pleasure Tulia gives reverberates in my cock.

"Suck deeply. Relax your throat."

She increases her suction, and I move one hand from her face to her hair, pushing my hips to reach her throat.

Tulia chokes, pauses to breathe, but then she holds me by the base and swallows me whole.

I watch her taking me, and the desire to subject her to the dirtiest fantasies intensifies.

"I want to fuck your mouth, but it won't be gentle."

She stops and looks at me.

"I think... huh... I don't like gentle."

Fuck, she's a delight.

"I don't think you understood, baby. I'm going to fuck you as if it were your sex."

Her eyes widen, but she nods.

Keiron lies back down and says to me:

"Hold on a bit. I want her to sit on my cock. I want to be buried in her up to the balls when you eat her mouth, but first, I'm going to suck her."

He pulls her up and sits her on his face.

"Spread your lips, beautiful," he says. "I'm going to make you come on my face."

While he's eating her out, I lean down and suck on her breasts.

Tulia has her eyes closed, trembling, and enjoying the sensation of being devoured by two men at once.

I lick and bite her nipples while Keiron fucks her relentlessly, and in a few seconds, she comes.

She looks at me just as her climax explodes, and while she's still lost in sensations, I stand up, hold her jaw to make her open her mouth, and enter her completely.

At the same time, Keiron slides her over his body, entering her pussy.

He makes her sit on his cock, and it takes us a few seconds to establish a rhythm inside her.

Tulia is giving herself completely, and I quickly forget that it's not just the two of us, focusing solely on her beautiful mouth engulfing me.

I stand on the sofa, to the side of Keiron, facing Tulia.

"Tilt your head back as far as you can. If you want to stop, just tell me."

She nods.

Like before, I hold her face, guiding, with the thrust of my hips, my cock into her warm mouth.

She moans and sucks, seeming eager to receive me.

"No foreplay this time, love. Make me come."

Keiron does something, and she moans, grinding on top of him, while at the same time welcoming me with her greedy mouth. I thrust a few times and I'm already very close to coming, like a damn teenager.

I force myself to slow down because I want to enjoy it a little longer.

She closes her eyes as if she's traveling in her own pleasure. Beautiful and surrendered. A fucking temptation.

I control the speed at which I fuck her so as not to scare her, going at a much slower pace than the desire I'm feeling.

Tulia accepts everything I give her, delivering what I demand.

I start to push faster, and she opens her eyes, looking unsure.

"Too much?"

She shakes her head, signaling no.

"I'm going to fuck you until I come, Tulia, but you need to know I won't stop even after that. I'm starving for you."

In sync with me, Keiron increases the intensity with which he's penetrating her, making her bounce on his lap.

The scene is fucking erotic, but even so, I want to tear her away and lock her in my room. I want to mark her entire body so that she doesn't crave another's pleasure, so that her beautiful face doesn't look ecstatic like it does now.

Fuck it! I must be going crazy.

I tilt her head back further, determined to block out these nonsensical thoughts.

I notice she's close to coming, both of them are, so I hold her hair in a firm grip, fucking her mouth relentlessly.

She moans around my cock as if she knows exactly what it takes to make me lose control completely.

I've never experienced such intense arousal from oral sex. Her moans as she sucks me and gets fucked simultaneously push me to the edge.

I fuck her, taking what I want, thrusting in and out of her throat, and when I feel myself growing in her mouth, I warn:

"I'm going to come, love."

Held captive by the pleasure she gives me, I hear Keiron shouting that he's coming from afar, while she trembles beneath me, reaching her climax as well.

My fingers grip her hair, and I pound her without stopping. Within seconds, I fill her mouth.

"Swallow it all."

I feel the jets of semen shooting from me and go crazy as I notice the movement of her throat while she obeys, drinking it down.

I empty myself inside her, but Tulia doesn't stop sucking me, cleaning me completely.

I'm not satisfied yet, and looking down, I see that Keiron's hands are on her hips, but neither of them is moving anymore.

"I'm taking her with me," I tell him and don't wait for a response, pulling Tulia off his lap.

I spread several pillows on the floor and lay her on the thick, plush carpet, over them.

I place another pillow under her ass and see a silent question on her face.

"I would never hurt you, baby, but I need to take you in every way. Every part of you."

I grab a condom and roll it onto my cock.

I lower myself between her thighs and enter her little pussy still wet with her fluids mixed with Keiron's. She moans, sensitive from the recent orgasm, but locks her legs around my back.

I suck on her breasts while pushing slowly, but I can't keep a gentle pace for long and then, I thrust all the way in, until my balls touch her pubes.

She bites me in response and I smile.

Our bodies fall into sync, and she's no longer just receiving. Now, Tulia demands everything from me too.

I thrust into her, and she grinds back.

I look between us, and the sight of her blonde-haired pussy opening to take me almost makes me explode.

I hold back because I want her to come for me first. Only then will I take her ass.

I rub her clit nonstop while sucking on her nipples, and with a cry of pleasure, she surrenders to a delicious orgasm.

I wait for her to relax and only then pull out of her, but Tulia hesitates to release her legs from around me.

"I need to prepare you, love."

She opens her mouth as if to say something, but then, understanding what I mean, closes it again, her cheeks turning very red.

I notice that Keiron has sat in an armchair near us, watching, while he masturbates.

He calls me and when I look, he tosses me the tube of lube.

"Your pussy is a paradise, but I'm dying to try that delicious ass."

I spin her around, positioning her on all fours, and place more pillows under her.

"Distract her," I tell Keiron, and with a smile, he kneels in front of Tulia's face. I stroke her hair. "We'll go at your pace, baby. You can stop me if I happen to cross any limits."

I switch to a new condom and apply a generous amount of lube to my finger, as well as to her virgin entry.

I play with her opening and she tightens up when I try to penetrate her, but she doesn't ask me to stop.

I'm delirious with desire, and when she moans for the first time since I started caressing her untouched spot, I begin to fuck her for real.

Keiron takes her mouth, filling it, and except for the fact that it's her ass I want, the position is very similar to the one we used in the bedroom.

She's slick with lube, and after the initial shock of the intrusion, she grinds back for me.

I insert another finger and she pushes back.

"Not yet, love. There's no need to feel more pain than necessary."

I spend several minutes letting her get used to me, but when she starts whining and reaches her hand to her thighs, I know I can't wait any longer.

I position the head of my cock at her ass and replace her hand with mine on her pussy, massaging her clit.

Tulia relaxes and I push a few centimeters into her tight passage.

She moans and, with her elbows resting on the ground, pulls Keiron's hips to take more of him.

I continue to push deeper.

Fuck, she's so hot and incredibly tight!

"I'm going to fuck you so good."

I slide two fingers into her pussy while my cock deepens into her virgin channel. As the head passes through, she screams but doesn't pull away.

"Beautiful," Keiron praises. "A man who can say you're his is one hell of a lottery winner, blonde."

He keeps fucking her mouth, but I stay still, working only my fingers on her pussy.

"Do you like it this way? Being taken in every way at the same time?" I ask.

She moans louder and when she wriggles her hips, offering herself, I bury myself completely in her.

Her whole body tenses, trying to push me out. I barely breathe, waiting for her to decide. I'm crazy with desire because even though she's in pain, Tulia clamps down and releases around me.

I caress her ass and seconds later, she seems focused on Keiron again.

I begin a steady rhythm, my hands gripping her waist like claws.

I fuck her at a consistent pace.

She accepts me, and I slide all the way in while my fingers delight in her wet folds.

"Tell me if it hurts."

I maintain a measured rhythm and only when I feel her clit throbbing, hard with desire, do I pull out and push back in deeper each time.

I lean in, bite her neck, and thrust firmly now, fucking her with care but increasing the speed with every stroke, my thumb working her clit.

She comes quickly, but I'm not ready to stop yet, so I lie down, bringing her with me.

Tulia gets startled.

"Shhh... I'll keep going without hurting you. Trust me."

I hold her thighs in my forearms, still buried in her, and hear a roar from Keiron.

"Fucking beautiful! I need to have you too, baby," he says.

Chapter 27

Tulia

I'm lying against his chest, feeling him completely inside me.

I've always associated anal sex with pain, but despite the initial discomfort, there was nothing but pleasure in the act.

Dominant yet tender, Rourke and Keiron have taken over each of my senses, overwhelming me with a lust that spilled over.

I always thought that being taken by two guys at once would make a woman feel used, like an object made for their pleasure.

That wasn't the case at all. Giving and receiving happened in perfect harmony. Our desire meeting halfway.

And now, when I should be dying of embarrassment for allowing myself to be possessed this way, I feel even more connected to both of them.

Will I have the courage to take this next step?

Rourke moves slowly inside me, nibbling on my ear, while Keiron approaches and kneels in front of us.

Rourke's legs are spread, his feet planted on the floor to push up, sinking deeper into my body.

It's not an easy slide, but it's incredibly pleasurable.

Without saying a word, Keiron touches my clit with his thumb. He massages it in circles, making my whole body hypersensitive.

"I need to be inside you, beautiful. I'm going slow, but I want to see you filled by both of us."

Instead of answering, I open my arms to him, and he smiles.

"I'll be right back."

I watch him put on a condom and am internally grateful for the care.

Rourke moves rhythmically beneath me, just to stay inside my body, but without startling me.

He licks my neck, sending shivers down my spine.

Keiron comes back and caresses my breasts, pinching my nipples.

"Come here," I call.

He positions himself at my sex and my breath catches in my throat.

Rourke doesn't let go of my thighs, keeping them open as if offering me to Keiron, who wraps his hands around my waist.

He brushes his slick lips before starting to push into me, slowly but with determination.

I whimper, scared, because I feel unbelievably stretched, and he pulls out.

"No rush," he promises.

Rourke's arms holding my legs are replaced by Keiron's, and soon I understand why: he now uses his hands to spread my ass cheeks and go deeper.

The first thrust makes me want to run away.

He doesn't insist. He bites and licks my ear.

"My sweet. You've given me everything, Tulia. I'm dying to come in this ass."

Fear gives way to desire and this time, when he enters and exits, I force myself to stay calm.

His constant pounding inside me slowly builds an intense wave of need, until I hear myself begging:

"More..."

"Oh, fuck!" he groans.

He's tense underneath me.

"Promise me you'll tell me if I'm hurting you, love. I'd rather lose an arm than hurt you."

"I promise."

Keiron is also fitted inside me, but not moving.

Rourke starts a slow rhythm, but with increasing voracity inside my body.

I can't control the loud moans of pleasure.

"You too," I ask Keiron, and with my plea, he takes me completely.

At first, everything is careful, slow, and sweet, but when we lock eyes, he seems to see something in my face; perhaps he noticed how powerful I feel, having both of them at my mercy, because he pulls out completely and then thrusts back in quickly and forcefully.

I think for a few seconds, all three of us stop breathing, dazed with pleasure.

When we resume, I gasp, my body delirious with small spasms, trembling with imminent climax.

"I..." I try to speak, but can't form a single sentence.

They understand, because Rourke bites my shoulder and starts pumping roughly, while Keiron caresses my clit, coming in and out of my sex as if he can't stop.

I'm the first to capitulate into an endless orgasm. Then, Keiron pulls out and, disposing of the condom, comes on my stomach.

Rourke lifts me, gently withdrawing from inside me, only to reposition me on my hands and knees once again.

He doesn't warn before reentering, his large hands gripping my hips.

He starts penetrating me with greed, even with a sting of pain, and I love his wildness.

Nothing makes me want to ask him to stop. It's exciting to know that I'm the one making him feel this way. The sensation of being dominated, of having my will subdued by him, surrendering to his pleasure, is leading me to another orgasm.

My body is his to do with as he pleases. Willingly, I offer him my submission.

"Fuck, Tulia," he shouts, gripping my waist.

Keiron moves closer and, as if they have a silent pact, strokes my clit. I almost jump with the combination of the burning in my ass and the sweet caress on my extremely sensitive bundle of nerves.

"Speed up. I'm going to come," Rourke warns him, groaning.

His fingers touch me as if I were an instrument he specializes in. I no longer have control over my body, and when Rourke is fully inside me, staying still, I succumb to a furious and devastating orgasm.

He resumes pumping until, finally, he yells my name, coming.

I collapse onto the cushions.

He pulls out slowly and, gathering me in his arms, lies down with me.

I barely notice when Keiron comes back and wraps me in a soft blanket.

He lies down too, positioning me between them, and for a few seconds, I feel that the mood has changed.

I look from one to the other and see them gazing at each other in silence.

Finally, Rourke allows his friend to hold me as well.

"Do you want anything? Water, food?" Rourke asks me.

"Sleep."

That's the last thing I remember saying before falling into a deep sleep.

I wake up hours later, feeling warm and protected, as muscular arms drape over my body.

I slip out of their hold and get up carefully.

My legs wobble as I stand, and for a moment of insanity, I think about returning to their warmth, but I can't afford to get used to them.

One is a man-whore, and the other is in love with his deceased wife.

Involving anything other than desire in this equation is a sure way to end up hurt.

Chapter 28

Tulia

I'm aware that I'm running away. I don't handle intimacy well in the short term.

I'm a person who likes rules and having them clearly established.

Dating is dating, hooking up is hooking up.

Casual sex is casual sex. Even if it's the kind that could shake the Earth's rotation.

Both are very engaging, and I'm too needy to keep my sanity in check when they both treat me like a queen.

"I'm not a pet that needs affection", I tell myself.

The anger I felt when I walked into the kitchen and heard Rourke talking about his ex-wife has passed.

It was overshadowed by the sensory overload of what happened next.

Although I don't believe I'll repeat the experience anytime soon, the feeling of being taken by two men at once is something I'll never forget.

The audacity to accept the indecent proposal, besides being driven by desire, of course, also came from irritation at Rourke seeming so sure he doesn't want a relationship, even though, according to his own words, the situation would be different if we weren't from rival organizations.

On the one hand, it was good because feeling challenged allowed me to let go in an experience that, without the right motivator, I might not have tried.

There's no trace of shyness left. I wanted to prove a point: that I could be as free within a casual relationship as anyone else.

Although I'm still not sure how the memories of what happened will affect me in the future, for now, I'm fine with my lessons in threesomes.

I enter the suite and head straight for the shower. Inside the stall, I rest my head against the wall, letting the water relax my body.

God, a woman who wants a long-term polyamorous relationship needs to be a gymnast.

I feel a slight discomfort in my ass, nothing too bothersome, but enough to remind me of what happened for a while.

I lather up under the water, caressing every spot they touched, reliving what happened.

Yes, I'm sore, but in a pleasant way.

Anal sex isn't something I've thought much about. After the first session with them, I realized I knew almost nothing. However, perhaps due to the situation, curiosity gradually found a place in my mind.

And it wasn't just that. I felt challenged by Rourke.

He thought I would run away, but what started as mutual provocation ended up turning into a kind of generator for sexual fantasies. I have a good stock of them for lonely nights from now on.

I turn off the shower, promising myself to enjoy this time with both of them without getting sentimental.

They both seem to come with a warning: *danger, don't fall in love.*

Keiron was right when he said that when the snowstorm is over, we'll have to move on without looking back.

I go back to the bedroom and collapse onto the bed, face down, without even taking off the towel.

I think I pass out from exhaustion because hours later, with the day already bright, I wake up to my phone ringing.

I squint my eyes, very tempted to ignore it, but I know from the music it's my sister, and she won't stop until I answer.

"*What were you doing?*" she asks, sounding suspicious as soon as I say hello.

Believe me when I say I'd rather not know, sis.

"Sleeping," I reply.

"*Are you at home?*"

"Is this an interrogation?" I say, suddenly awake and sitting on the bed.

"*No, I just wanted to know if you were working because of the snowstorm that hit the country.*

"I'm safe." I offer a half-truth.

With two men who would make her green with envy.

"*I want to confirm that you really won't come to my son's birthday.*"

My nephew is the only boy in families where only girls are born from both of our parents, and I adore him. It hurts so much not to have him around anymore.

I let myself fall back onto the bed again.

"No, I'm not coming."

"*Do you want to know something, Tulia? Everyone is sick of your pathetic attempt to get attention.*"

"Attempt to get attention? What the hell are you talking about?"

"*I know exactly what you're doing. You were the favorite daughter, but you know you were sidelined after you acted like a selfish brat, leaving everything behind on the eve of your wedding.*"

"You have no idea what you're talking about, Alla. Maybe if you tried taking your head out of the sand like an ostrich, you'd see more around you."

"*What I see is a twenty-three-year-old woman acting like a little girl. You're making our parents suffer with your absence. They can't even enjoy the parties anymore because it feels like your ghost is here, Tulia. At least come once and tell them you don't want to be part of our lives anymore. After that, you can disappear forever!"*

I get up and pace around the room while listening to her, struggling not to cry.

I try to convince myself that everything she's saying is due to ignorance.

Alla has no clue what I've seen, but it doesn't matter because I still hate her just the same at this moment.

They're suffering from my absence? And what about me, who has no one to celebrate my birthday with?

I would never be as cruel as she's being without knowing both sides of the story.

The problem is that if I tell them, I'll destroy my family.

"I have to go," I say.

"That's right. Run away. It's what you do best."

"No, you're mistaken, sister. It was what I needed to do to keep from going insane. As for wanting attention, you couldn't be more wrong. All I want is to forget the past, but every time you torment me, it comes back."

I'm sobbing, and I hate her for it.

Since I've been on my own, after leaving my town, I've been too hard on myself and can't afford to show any vulnerability.

"Tell me," she says, changing her tone.

"One day," I reply. "Don't call me again if it's to ask me to come back home. It's not going to happen."

I hang up the phone and run to the bathroom. I lean over the counter intending to wash my face, but the crying comes even harder.

I think it's anger at myself for breaking down in front of her.

I don't know how much time passes. I don't realize I'm not alone until I feel strong arms around me.

"No," I protest, but I don't even know against what.

When he turns me around, he holds me even tighter against his chest.

I grunt, but Rourke doesn't care about my objections. He picks me up and carries me back to the bedroom, sitting on the bed. He leans back with me wrapped in his embrace.

Chapter 29

Rourke

I didn't intend to come after her.

I wanted to be alone for a bit to process what happened during the night, trying to sort out my fucked-up thoughts. But it was as if a magnet was pulling me; my feet led me to her room.

The door was open, so I didn't bother announcing myself.

I'm not sure what I expected when I went looking for her, but it certainly wasn't to find her crying in the bathroom.

"What happened, baby?"

"Nothing. Let me go," she asks after I carry her to the bed.

"No."

"I don't need to be taken care of."

"Believe me, I'm terrible at taking care of someone. But hugging, that I know how to do. Now tell me why you were crying."

"My sister called me."

"And what's the big deal? You don't get along?"

"We were never best friends, if that's what you're asking, but we weren't enemies either. Since I left home, though, every time we talk, we fight. I don't even know why she still calls me."

"Probably because she misses you."

"I don't believe that. I think she's bothered that I escaped the confined upbringing we had."

"Was it really that bad?" I ask, wiping a tear that has rolled down her cheek.

She looks at me as if she's about to snarl, and despite my best effort, I smile.

"You're unbelievable, Russian. Ready for a fight at any moment."

Deep down, I know why she's upset with me. It's a conscious effort. She wants to break the intimacy. The invisible bond we never wanted, but which has created a connection between us from the start.

"A bond of three," a voice warns, but I ignore it.

"Don't think just because we've been intimate that we're friends. You're from the rival organization."

I bend down and whisper in her ear:

"Keep telling yourself that. We're much more than friends. I've had you in every way a man can have a woman, Tulia."

"It wasn't very gentlemanly of you to remind me of that."

"As if you could have forgotten. Lie to me, girl. Say you don't still feel me inside your body."

As I expected, she pulls away, which, in my current state, is a good thing.

I had to hold her for less than five minutes in my lap to get as hard as steel. Considering what happened just a few hours ago, I think I might need to start worrying about becoming a sex addict.

Or addicted to her.

"You're very arrogant, Irish."

Tulia keeps resisting me because I think she prefers to fight than to surrender to our attraction. I understand because I feel the same way.

When Keiron is around, it's easier to ignore the urge I have to lock her up somewhere and keep the sassy blonde all to myself. Maybe the same thing is happening inside her.

"Tell me why you fought with your sister," I insist, bringing up a neutral topic.

"It's a long story and I don't like to confide in people, but to sum up, no one in my family knows what happened for me to leave, and that's why my sister keeps insisting I visit them."

"If you don't share, as you said, how do you deal with what hurts you?"

"How do you know there's something that hurts me?"

Because a broken person recognizes another.

"You ended an engagement and never visited your family again. You don't have to be a genius to put two and two together. We probably won't see each other again after this snowfall. Taisiya won't be able to visit Lorcan forever, and thus, your job will be done."

"It's not about whether you'll tell someone, it's because I don't like to remember that day."

"The day it was snowing and you ran away?"

She nods, agreeing.

"Share it with me, Russian."

I'm not one to insist people confess personal details, but I can recognize pain, and there's a lot of it inside her.

"I was betrayed practically on the eve of my wedding."

"Yeah, I knew that. You dodged a bullet marrying an ass. It's the only explanation for the idiot to have betrayed you."

She hides a smile.

"You have a unique talent for making me hate you and like you a little at the same time, Rourke."

"It's not an empty compliment, Tulia. You're beautiful. Any man who doesn't value you as his queen doesn't deserve you."

"Well, Simeon didn't and he did it spectacularly. I came home and found him fucking someone in our suite."

"Fuck!"

"What did you do?"

"Nothing. I'd heard that people, when faced with traumatic situations, go into shock. They freeze, unable to act. I proved that true for myself. I didn't speak, didn't cry. I just watched the two of them, unable to believe it."

"Was it someone you knew? A bridesmaid? A friend?"

She stands up and walks to the window, turning her back to me.

"He betrayed me with my father."

At first, I think I didn't hear her correctly, so I walk over to her and turn her to face me.

"I thought you said your fiancé betrayed you with your father."

Tulia doesn't respond, and gradually, from the look on her face, I see that there was no mistake.

"Fuck me! They were lovers?"

She looks down at her feet.

"I don't know when it started. I have no idea if they were involved before we started dating, since they're both from the Organization, or if the relationship began afterward. Shortly after I ran away, I almost went crazy trying to guess the answers, but after a while, I realized it didn't matter. They both betrayed me."

"I don't know what to say to you."

"There's nothing to say. My hurt isn't because it was another man. It would have hurt just as much if he'd been cheating with one of my future bridesmaids. But with my father, the man who contributed to my existence, it nearly destroyed me. When people learn something like that, they usually run to their family for comfort. Aside from the cousin who took me in, I had no one, no family shoulder to cry on."

"You didn't tell your mother or sister the truth," I say, stating the obvious. If she had revealed the betrayal, her sister wouldn't be insisting she come home.

"No, and I don't even know if I ever will. My mother is an older version of who I used to be. She wouldn't know how to live without my father."

"Even if that means living within a lie?"

"Some people prefer lies to harsh realities."

"Maybe, but not you."

"Never. As I said, even if it were with another woman, I would never forgive him, but the fact that it was with a relative, the man who helped bring me into existence, it almost killed me."

I pull her into my arms, and this time, she doesn't resist. I kiss her hair, having no idea how to comfort someone in such a situation.

"What the hell were they thinking, Rourke? To carry that on for years? To continue the charade without caring about the lives they were destroying? They left me with nowhere to go. In one day, I lost everything. My father and the man I loved."

"I wouldn't go back home either if I were in your place."

She cries even more and remains that way for several minutes.

When I feel her relax, I pick her up and carry her back to bed.

"What do you think you're doing?"

"Taking you to sleep."

"I'm not a baby. Besides, it's the middle of the morning."

"And who cares, Russian? Now, be quiet."

Chapter 30

Rourke

I should let her go, but I don't want to just yet. Aside from Keiron, I haven't felt this connected to someone since Viona died.

I don't allow myself to think too deeply about why, blaming the fact that Tulia was the woman for whom I broke years of celibacy, so I guess it's natural that a bond formed between us.

She's snoring in my arms, but even so, she doesn't fully relax, typical of people who don't know how to trust.

Who could blame her? Her story seems like a fucked-up nightmare. Double betrayal by people she loved.

I see movement near the door, and when I lift my head, I realize it's Keiron.

How long has he been watching us?

I carefully lift her off my body, and after laying her down, I cover her with the duvet.

I walk towards him. When I reach the hallway, I close the door behind me.

"Keeping me out?"

"What's your problem?"

"Mine? None. From where I'm standing, you're up to your neck in one."

"I don't know what you're talking about."

I head downstairs with no intention of talking.

I enter the kitchen and start the coffee maker, but when I look back, I realize he followed me.

"Are you pissed about what happened? We all wanted it."

"No, Keiron, I'm not. If there's anyone I'd share a woman with in this fucked-up life, it's you."

"Then what's the problem?"

How can I answer him?

I shake my head and plant both hands on the counter. The same one where, just a few hours ago, my Russian was sprawled, waiting to receive the pleasure she deserves.

"Rourke, what the hell is going on?"

"I don't want to feel possessive about her. I don't want to feel, damn it!"

"It's not exactly something you can choose."

"And what do you know about that? Your relationships last as long as a good fuck!"

"And I'm fine with them being that way. But you, my friend, if you want an opinion, you're a one-woman man, and apparently, contrary to what you think, your heart, not your cock, has already chosen someone."

I give up on getting the coffee and start leaving the kitchen.

"Rourke..."

"I told you before: even if she wasn't the enemy, I'm not looking for a relationship."

"If what you want with Tulia is just a fuck, which I doubt very much, you'd better be quick. They just announced on the app that tomorrow morning the streets will be cleared. She'll be gone forever soon."

I feel my jaw clench. The tension, already present in my body, triples.

"We knew it would happen sooner or later."

"Yeah, so I guess we'd better make the most of the little time we have left with our blonde."

I growl as soon as he says "our blonde," and the bastard laughs.

"Go upstairs, Rourke. I'm not a fucking marriage counselor. I don't understand relationships, but anyone can see that Tulia is taking over every inch of your brain, or you wouldn't have broken celibacy."

It's on the tip of my tongue to repeat that it's just sex, but I can't. Not after having possessed her in every way.

I turn my back on him and nearly run up the stairs, all the while hearing a damn clock ticking in my head, warning me that starting tomorrow, Tulia will be out of my world.

This time, when I enter her room, I close the door. Not because I think Keiron will come, but in an attempt to isolate us from the world.

I walk to the window and notice that the snow has melted considerably.

I approach the bed and spend a long time looking at her asleep, thinking about everything that has happened since we arrived at this apartment.

I didn't lie when I told Keiron that I'm not angry with him.

How could I, when what happened between us was mutual attraction from the start? Something changed along the way, though.

The dislike that she and I felt for each other, I now understand, is the result of intense sexual attraction and something more: like recognizes like.

We're both broken inside. Maybe beyond any chance of repair.

"Rourke?" she asks, opening her eyes.

For a few seconds, I just keep looking at her. She no longer has the duvet covering her. The towel has come undone, and she's completely naked.

She doesn't look at me anymore like the confident blonde from a few hours ago. She looks sweet and sleepy.

Vulnerable.

Maybe the person she was before her heart was broken.

"What do you do when you're alone?"

"What?"

"On holidays, at the end of the year. Who do you stay with? You can't go back to your family."

I don't say this to hurt her, but suddenly, the question seems important to me.

Starting tomorrow, I won't be able to know anything more about her.

She sits up in bed as if I've given her a jolt.

"No one. I don't need company."

"The snow is melting."

"You're not making sense, Rourke."

"Starting tomorrow, it's over."

I watch her swallow hard as she sees me climbing onto the bed.

"I haven't had enough of you yet."

I don't touch her but lean toward her, making her lie down.

I'm hovering over her body, one arm on each side of her face.

"And what do you want to do to fix that?"

"Stay inside you until the moment we leave."

She raises her hand and touches my jaw.

"And Keiron?"

"Do you want me to call him?"

"No. I want you."

Chapter 31

Tulia

My heart pounds frighteningly in my chest.

Thump. Thump. Thump.

It's not a rhythmic thudding; it's uncontrolled; and control, in my world of solitary survival, is the key word.

I should push him away because Rourke's eyes are telling me much more than his words ever could.

I don't, though. I throw caution to the wind and give in to what every part of me is begging for: hours in his arms.

It's not a need I handle easily. It frightens me, but it can't be tamed. So, the moment I feel his broad, calloused fingers on my neck, I surrender to the kiss, letting him take over my mouth as he has with my body every time he touched me.

There's no clothing in the way, except for the boxer he's wearing, so when he spreads my thighs to fit us together, I feel the full length of his hardness against my bare sex.

My nipples are erect, tight with desire, just like the rest of my body. Rourke lowers his face, leisurely caressing one and then the other with his lips.

"Don't make love to me. Fuck me," I beg.

I can deal with the memories of a few nights of wild sex when I have to say goodbye. As satisfied as my body has been with the possession of both of them, that's all I, he, and Keiron have had so far.

I don't know if I'll survive, however, the memory of his gaze on me in this moment.

"It doesn't matter what name we give it, Tulia. I've never wanted a woman as much as I want you."

I'm not sure if he knows what he's saying, and I want to ask him to stop, not to tell me something that will feed my hungry heart for love.

I pull his mouth to mine and give him a hard, voracious kiss. I bite his lips, showing that there are no feelings involved. It's pure carnal desire.

Rourke tightens his grip on my hair, controlling my movements. In contrast to the rough tenderness, he kisses my mouth deeply and intensely, his tongue working inside me, exploring every corner. Tasting me and making me moan, begging for more.

He slides kisses down my neck and breasts. He stops to give attention to each one, his tongue circling the nipples, sucking and licking as if he can't get enough of what he needs to satisfy himself.

He reaches my stomach but doesn't go lower to the juncture between my thighs. He spends a moment caressing my navel with his tongue, then nibbles at the mound of Venus, and only when I think I might die if I don't feel his tongue on me, does he give me what I want.

Rourke

TULIA'S FACE IS FLUSHED with excitement. Her lips are swollen and wet, and with every touch of my tongue on her body, she seems breathless.

The desire I feel for her is fierce, untamed, but this time, I want to savor her carefully. Imprint her on me.

Fingers, hands, nails, tongue, and cock memorizing every inch of her.

I know that while I explored her body, caressing her leisurely, she was anxious, but I don't want her to only feel pleasure. I want her to *feel me*.

I part her wet folds with my fingers, and when I trap her clit between my teeth, pulling gently, her hands come to my hair.

"Rourke..."

"I'm getting addicted to those moans, my blonde."

She's drenched, her honey dripping from the tiny opening; I bite and suck the sweet flesh, my tongue swirling over her sex in circular motions.

Her pleasure-filled squeals fuel my madness, and I suck her hot pussy with my mouth open, inserting a finger in motions similar to a fuck.

She writhes, restless, filthy, crazy with arousal.

I grip her hips, holding her still, and continue my relentless assault on her sex.

"I could spend the rest of my days with my face buried in this pussy."

I insert another finger into her opening and return to sucking her clit. Tulia whimpers, begging me not to stop.

I couldn't even if I wanted to. I'm starving and feast on her sex until she finally gives me her orgasm, filling my mouth.

I rise up, positioning myself inside her. I don't enter yet. I grip her hair and pull her into a kiss.

Breathless, our tongues devour each other with need, a confrontation that is also an invitation for mutual possession.

"Are you in pain?"

She blushes.

"Just a little, but I need you inside me."

"Touch yourself while I fuck you. I want to hear your moans every time I bury myself in your pussy."

I lift one of her legs onto my shoulder. She's spread wide open, and after testing just the tip of my thick head between her lips, I push in all the way.

"Oh, God..."

Fitting inside her never happens easily, even when she's so wet. With my elbows resting on her sides, I kiss her mouth to make her relax for me.

I circle a nipple with my tongue, then pull it with my teeth.

I pound into her again and again, and soon we're soaked with sweat.

She writhes and I squeeze her ass, starting a faster rhythm. Tulia moves with me, begging for me to go deeper, harder, scratching my back and shoulders.

The loss of control takes over both of us, and without caring that what we have is temporary, oaths and promises are whispered by both.

I don't know how much time passes, I lose myself in the void of our lust, but when Tulia starts to raise her hips to meet mine, her pussy contracting and releasing in regular spasms, I start to fuck her with brutality.

She pulls me close, whispers in my ear that she's going to come for me, and it drives me wild.

I flick her pleasure point, and when she lets out a moan of pure ecstasy, her sex convulsing around my cock like a wild animal, I enter one last time and come, spilling my semen from her.

I focus back on her mouth because I can't let her go yet.

She kisses me back as if I were the air in her lungs, moaning my name.

I pull away to look at her.

A lock of hair covers her beautiful face and I tuck it behind her ear, trying to tell myself that we'll be fine with the end because we knew it was temporary, but Tulia's eyes stop me from accepting that.

There's a silent plea in them.

One that we both know she shouldn't make, but that I can't ignore.

She wraps her arms around my neck but doesn't kiss me, just stays very close, feeling me, breathing me in.

"I don't want it to end," she says.

Something hot like lava spreads through my chest, making me even more fascinated by her. By her courage to put into words what we both want.

"I don't want it to end either."

Tulia

WHEN I WAKE UP HOURS later, the room is in that type of darkness that precedes dawn.

I feel exhausted, and the reason is that we barely slept, searching for each other all night.

We didn't talk again about trying to stay together, but each time we made love, I felt the connection between us grow.

I turn to my side and watch him. Rourke is lying on his stomach, his naked and tattooed body sprawled across the bed. One leg is bent and his arm is draped over my stomach, holding me close.

He murmurs something in his sleep, and at first, I smile, trying to guess if he's dreaming about me, but then I hear him clearly say:

"Forgive me, Viona. I wish I could go back in time."

My mind tries to play tricks on me, swearing he didn't say that, but the phrase repeats, and now there's a pained expression on his sleeping face.

I feel a chill inside, the need to flee growing with an uncontrollable wave.

I get out of bed and, without stopping to think, head to the bathroom where Keiron had left the clothes I arrived in, already clean and dry.

I quickly dress and grab my backpack from the armchair.

When I reach the door, I feel an almost irresistible urge to look back, to see him one last time, but I don't allow myself to.

Chapter 32

Keiron

"**W**hy are you running away?" I ask as she already has her hand on the doorknob, almost leaving the apartment.

Tulia turns to me and, although her face no longer shows the anger she pretended to feel after discovering that we were part of the Syndicate, she also doesn't seem like the woman who came multiple times *with me* and *for me* in the past few days.

Her face gives no clue about what she's feeling. She looks at me with no emotion, like a blank slate.

I'm not getting it. I know Rourke went to her room last night and didn't come out, which means they spent the night together.

I'm not the type to believe in romance, but I thought they might manage some sort of arrangement, a chance meeting, or whatever the hell, because it's clear they don't want to say goodbye yet.

Her stance doesn't indicate that, however.

"I'm not running away. I'm leaving."

"Without saying goodbye?"

I take a step closer, and what could have frightened her instead seems to disarm her.

"I need to go, Keiron."

"I'm not needy. I wouldn't be pissed if you left without saying goodbye, but what about Rourke?"

"He's sleeping."

I raise my arms in surrender.

I know better than anyone how fucked up it is to be forced into confessions.

"Alright, baby. Do what's best for you. Now come here and give me a hug."

I don't give her time to protest, pulling her against my body and pressing our foreheads together.

"I kind of love you a little now, Russian. It was a good snowstorm," I say, giving her a wink.

She hides a smile and shrugs.

"I don't hate snow that much anymore."

I hold her chin.

"Are you sure you don't want to wait for Rourke to wake up?"

She takes a moment before answering, and when she does, her lips are trembling.

"It would never work, Keiron. We're part of rival organizations."

"You're not a coward, pretty. If you really wanted to, you'd find a way."

She looks at my chest.

"He said her name in his sleep."

Fuck me!

"Whose name?" I ask, playing dumb because above all, I'm loyal to my friend.

"I think it was his wife's. *Viona*."

"Oh, fuck, baby."

I pull her head to my chest, but this time, she pulls away.

"I'm leaving. Thanks... huh... for sheltering me from the snow."

I can't even form a sentence, and she's already gone.

Who wouldn't run away in her place?

"WHERE'S TULIA?" ROURKE asks about an hour later.

"She left. The snowstorm is over, my friend."

He's only in his underwear, which tells me he must have run down as soon as he woke up and didn't find her.

"Not for me."

"What are you planning to do with her, Rourke? I don't need to explain that the risk of both of you dying if you stay together is high, right?"

"Lorcan is with the Russian nun. I'll find a way too."

"Man, if Cillian doesn't have both of you killed, Yerik will."

He starts heading up the stairs.

"Did she say she'd be back home?"

"No. She didn't say anything other than that she was leaving."

I'm not about to get into the fact that she mentioned Viona's name in her sleep. Rourke already carries the guilt of his ex-wife's death. He doesn't need to add to it.

"Why does it seem like you're trying to make me give up on finding her? You didn't think like this yesterday, but you know what? I don't care. I'm going to find her."

"Have you considered that maybe you're not ready yet? She's already been broken. She doesn't deserve to be a stand-in for your deceased wife."

"Fuck you, Keiron. You have no idea what you're talking about."

"Explain it to me."

He stops and runs his hands through his hair.

"I want her."

"For how long? You need to think about it, Rourke. Even if Cillian agrees to another Russian switching sides, Yerik won't let his women start defecting and becoming our partners. Your relationship can't be a regular affair. If you want Tulia, it has to be for a commitment. Be sure about that decision before taking such a big step."

"I don't need to think. I've been alone for four years because no one could melt the ice inside me. She went beyond that. She spread through my bloodstream."

"Don't kill me for asking this, but aren't you confusing lust with passion?"

"I'm not driven by desire, Keiron. I was celibate for years. I broke the fast with her and only with her. Tulia struck me deeply."

I shake my head, smiling.

"You'll be like Romeo and Juliet of modern times. The difference is you won't need to commit suicide in the end. There are two mafias ready to give you both a 'forever,' but six feet under."

"Nothing will happen. I'll talk to Lorcan. He'll understand."

As if he had guessed we were talking about him, both our phones ring, and we know who's calling.

"Yes, boss." I'm the first to answer.

"The snow is over. We have a mission in two days."

"Where to?"

"An island."

He doesn't explain further, hanging up immediately.

"What's going on?"

"We have a trip the day after tomorrow. Fuck, I need to talk to her before anything else. I'm starting to understand how Tulia's mind works. She's become an expert at running away. I don't know what made her leave, but I think she might have feared the complications we'd face together."

"I don't believe it was just that. She's not a coward."

"I know what I saw in her eyes in the early morning. Tulia said she wasn't ready to let me go. She wouldn't just change her mind."

"Then go after her, but be discreet. Remember, Tulia isn't just a Russian soldier; she's a soldier hated by the wife of one of Yerik's trusted men. There's definitely someone watching her."

Tulia

Hours earlier

"I NEED A FEW DAYS OFF, Taisiya," I say on the phone, after confirming that she's fine and will return to the convent in a few hours.

"Are you going to visit your family?"

"No, but I need a week to rest."

"Did something happen... huh... during the snowstorm?"

"No. Everything's fine, boss. Just let me know if I can take those days off."

"You can. I'll talk to Ana, and she'll inform Maxim." She pauses before continuing. "You know if you need to talk, I'm here, right?"

"Okay. Thanks. Bye."

I hang up the phone, and after a quick shower, I decide to get moving. I pack some clothes into my backpack and leave the house. The worst that can happen is Maxim saying "no" and me having to come back.

I'm not a prisoner.

If things get complicated due to my unplanned escape, Taisiya will intervene on my behalf. I don't like the idea of being in anyone's debt, but I need to be isolated for a while.

Keiron

"SHE'S NOT HERE, ROURKE. She's left the city," I say, knocking on his car window.

When he unlocks the door, I walk around and sit in the passenger seat while I watch Tulia's building.

"How do you know that?"

"Through the quickest route: I asked Taisiya. Tulia took a few days off."

"Why?"

I know he's not asking about the vacation but why she disappeared without saying goodbye.

I lean back in the seat and close my eyes. I promised myself I wouldn't get involved, but even though I like the blonde a lot, my loyalty belongs to Rourke.

"You said Viona's name in your sleep."

"Oh, fuck!"

"She's been betrayed once. I doubt she wants to be someone's second choice."

"She wasn't just betrayed; she was hurt by two people she loved."

He quickly tells me the reason she fled from her family, a story that takes me a few minutes to process. A betrayal is already something pretty fucked up to digest, which is why I never get into relationships: I'm incapable of being faithful. Betrayal within a family, however, must be a fucking nightmare.

"Did she say what I was saying in my sleep?"

"Yes. You were asking Viona not to leave you. She's hurt, Rourke, and if you really want her, there's only one way to fix things: tell the truth about your wife's death."

Chapter 33

Tulia

I look at my mother and sister through the phone screen and at this moment, I'm sure that my bond with them has been completely severed.

After four days away from Boston, I mustered the courage to go back to my hometown to finally clear up the past. To talk, including with my father.

I concluded that I couldn't run away forever.

A guardian angel, I suppose, advised me to call ahead, so I stayed at a hotel in a nearby town and invited them, via message, for a video call.

It took just a few minutes of talking with them to realize that nothing would ever be fixed between us.

Alla said she went after Simeon after our last call and that he *confessed* that he caught me with someone else in our future home.

According to her, that's why I ran away: *I* had betrayed him.

With a look of disdain, she and my mother said that Daddy confirmed the *truth*. Even after betraying me, he was still capable of maintaining such a charade.

Despite the pain, it wasn't the fact that they lied to me that disappointed me. It was how quickly the two of them were convinced.

As I watch them, I wonder when in my life I showed that I was capable of such a thing. I've always been well-behaved, the perfect daughter.

And then, suddenly, I become the villain?

"Aren't you going to say anything?" my sister asks.

I try to keep a neutral face, but I know I can't. Not in front of them. I was stupid enough to think there was a chance to have at least part of my family back, and now I hate myself for feeling hope.

I doubt that even if I denied their claims and told the truth, they would believe me.

They need to believe that the world they live in actually exists. A place where everything is perfect. I am the discordant element in this story.

"Have a good life. I love you, Mom."

I hang up before they can respond, determined to talk to Taisiya about my future. If there's anyone who can help me, it's her.

I'm confused about many things, but there is one thing clear as the sunrise each day: I don't want to continue in the Organization.

Now I realize that I made the worst mistake of my life by joining. It's not about judging who's involved. I grew up in this environment and accept people as they are. It's just not what I want for myself personally.

I go online to buy a plane ticket and return home. My real home, this time. I have nothing left to do here.

I ran away from Boston, but I don't want to run from anything in life anymore.

It's time to admit that I'm an adult.

Two Days Later

"DID YOU MANAGE TO STAY well during the blizzard?" Taisiya asks when I go to visit her at the convent shortly after returning to Boston. "You didn't mention anything about the days you had to spend in the company of the *enemies*, as you called them."

I make a tremendous effort not to let my cheeks flush, but I think I fail because she hides a smile.

We are walking outside the convent, and the day is beautiful, sunny, and the temperature is finally starting to feel like spring.

I don't feel springlike at all. In my lonely mind and heart, it is still winter.

"They're not as bad as I thought," I say, without committing myself.

She stops walking and looks at me.

"I'm going to have to disagree. They are pretty bad. After all, they're mobsters, just like you."

"You're quite a peculiar nun."

"Maybe because I'm not a nun yet," she replies, and I almost laugh because it seems to me that in her mind, she's giving me lip for being so nosy.

"Something tells me you'll never become one."

"I don't know what you're talking about."

"I'm not stupid, Taisiya."

"If you're not as stupid as you say, don't stick your nose where it doesn't belong; it could be bad for you. Next time you irritate someone like you did with Sierra, you might end up being sent to Siberia."

"Are you threatening me?"

"Me? Far from it. I'm just a mere novice."

"You're pretty sharp, that's for sure."

"Ah, I can't deny that. Unlike you, who earned the eternal hatred of Leonid's wife. Anastacia told me that Sierra can't even hear your name."

"I was on a mission, following orders."

"How unfortunate, then, that your *mission* turned out to be the first lady of one of Pakhan's trusted men."

I shake my head, smiling. So much has happened since I earned Leonid's wife's hatred as a bonus that it has become a minor issue.

"Yes, I'm the unluckiest rookie in the world. Did you know Sierra was my first job?"

"Uh-huh. If someone looks up the word 'unlucky' in the dictionary, I'm sure your photo will appear."

She resumes walking, and I follow her.

"I like you, Taisiya. I don't know what your life has been like up to now, because no one goes into detail about how you ended up in the United States, but from what I know, I really like you, and that's why I'm going to give you a piece of advice: I hope you know what you're doing."

She knows I'm talking about her involvement with Lorcan.

"And I'll give you one in return: be careful with what you say, Tulia. I don't want to hurt you with my problems. I might get into trouble, but I'll always be Ana's sister. Maxim would never let anything bad happen to me, but if they find out you're somehow connected with the guys..."

"I know," I say, because it has crossed my mind millions of times.

In all of them, I had to push away the voice that said that if Rourke weren't still in love with his deceased wife, he would be a man worth fighting for, and I would bid farewell to the Organization without any doubts to be with him.

I've blocked out any thoughts about the blizzard days in my heart. I don't feel ashamed of what happened between the three of us. I enjoyed it. However, the end was a bucket of cold water.

I didn't expect him to say he was in love with me, but hearing him call out his ex-wife's name right after we confessed that we didn't want what we had to end, took me to a place in my mind where I no longer want to be: the second choice in someone's life.

"Do you want to talk about it?" she asks.

"No, thank you. I don't even know why I came here."

Actually, I do know. It's to ask to be released as your bodyguard.

I know that by staying with Taisiya, I'll be protected from Sierra's hatred, but seeing Rourke again will hurt me.

"Maybe you needed to talk."

"Yes, maybe, but you're right about one thing: we can't talk about the present. It would be dangerous for both of us."

"And the past?" she asks.

"No, I don't want to talk about the past."

"Alright. Can you answer basic questions, then? We sound like two secret agents talking."

"I suppose we're almost that. Go ahead and ask your question."

"Were you born here in Boston?"

"No. In the central United States. My parents, however, are Russian."

"And where are they?"

"Together."

"Far from you? Don't you see them?"

I shake my head in the negative.

"Do you have siblings?"

"A married sister and a cousin who is almost like a sister."

I omit the fact that Sierra hates Fanya as much as she hates me.

"I'm sorry if I'm being intrusive, it's just that..." She suddenly stops talking and if I hadn't been quick, she would have fallen to the ground.

"Taisiya, are you okay?"

"No, I'm not. Take me to my sister's house, but please, for everything that is holy, don't report this to Maxim."

She looks like she's about to faint, and this time it's not from dizziness, but from fear. I pull her into a hug.

"What's this? I don't know what you're talking about. As far as I know, you missed Anastacia. That's all."

I ACCOMPANIED HER TO her brother-in-law Maxim's house, one of Pakhan's four trusted men and as scary as hell.

I've never seen Dmitri and Grigori in person, but Leonid, whom I already know, at least gives you the false sense that he won't kill you. Anastacia's husband, however, looks at you as if he were observing a wall. He shows no emotion.

It's as if there's no soul within him.

I didn't just leave her here. I stayed all day because I wanted to make sure Taisiya was truly okay. She locked herself in the room with her sister for a long time, and after the doctor examined her, she dropped two bombs on me: she confessed she's pregnant by the Irishman and also that, with her sister's help, she's going to the boss of the Syndicate's family home.

Jesus, a war is about to explode, I'm sure of it. There's no way the two bosses will agree to something like this.

She also revealed that she has fully recovered her memory and I have no idea what that means, but I guess it can't be good because the girl seems wounded in her soul.

I don't even know why she told me all this, but now I feel responsible for Taisiya. I need to make sure she'll be okay.

I knock on the bedroom door and wait for her to authorize me to enter.

Anastacia isn't there, and I breathe a sigh of relief.

"How are you feeling?"

"I'm exhausted," she says, already dressed and ready, I'm sure, to go to Cillian's aunt's house.

"Are you really going to stay with the Irish?"

"I have to go, Tulia. I need to think about my baby."

I nod, agreeing.

Lorcan will protect her above all else.

"And you, will you be okay?"

"Girl, you have problems up to your soul and you're worried about me?"

"You seem sad."

"Yes, and I am, but I don't want to burden you any further."

"Talk to me, Tulia."

"I don't even know where to start."

"I'm a good listener."

"How much time do you have?"

She looks at the watch on her wrist.

"About an hour. Now talk."

I sit beside her and for the first time, narrate my story, mainly what happened that made me run away from home, with a beginning, middle, and end, not the summarized version I gave to Rourke.

I think that because she is a woman, I feel more embraced. Taisiya will understand exactly how I felt.

"Was that why you joined the Organization?" she asks when I finish.

"Yes. And I'm really damn sorry."

I know that what I've just said could mean my death sentence, but if there's anyone who can help me, it's her.

"And in all this story of regret, is there an Irish soldier involved or..." she pauses, "both?"

"It's not about them that I want to leave the Organization. It's for myself. As for my relationship with the guys, I'm not going to tell you about that, but yes, only one of them touches my heart."

"Oh my God! What have I done?"

"I didn't understand."

"If it weren't for me, you'd never have met either of them."

"I had already met them in a bar before."

"Seriously? I'm relieved to know that. Ana would say it was your destiny, then."

"I don't know and I don't care. It's over. What I came to talk to you about is helping me get out of the Brotherhood."

She pales.

"It's impossible!" she responds, voicing my biggest fear.

"I don't know what to do."

She holds my hands.

"Let me get to Aunt Orla's house and I'll think of something. For now, keep a low profile. Don't be upset, but I've already taken the liberty of asking my sister to look out for you while I'm away."

"What do you mean?"

"I thought you were going to run away with the soldiers."

I laugh, thinking she's joking.

She's not, I realize in seconds.

"Was I that obvious?"

"Being around you guys was like getting close to an electric power plant, with all the energy flowing from the attraction."

"But that was all it was: attraction. Then, it turned into something more."

"With which one?"

"Rourke."

She looks surprised.

"The widower?"

I shrug.

"As I said, it's over."

"I shouldn't be telling you this, but they're on a mission."

"What?"

"It's something dangerous, and I'm only telling you because if it were about Lorcan, I'd want to know."

"Can you let me know if they're okay once you find out?"

"They?"

"Regardless of my feelings for Rourke, I care about Keiron too."

"I'll let you know, don't worry."

"You shouldn't be a nun but a saint, Taisiya. How do you manage to think of others even when you're pregnant by an Irishman and about to run away to the boss of the Syndicate's aunt's house?"

"I don't think about everyone. Just the people I care about. I'll talk to my sister. If there's a chance to get you out of the Organization, I'll do it."

Chapter 34

Rourke

Death has been a part of my life since I was a kid. I come from a family of mobsters, like most of the guys admitted as members of the Syndicate.

I killed for the first time at fifteen, and since then, I haven't stopped.

It's just another job. I consider myself a kind of hell's delivery man, sending the souls of enemies to Satan.

However, today's mission will stay in my memory forever.

We didn't have the illusion of finding the girls we came to rescue smiling and healthy. They had lived for years in the hands of a damn pedophile lawyer who was one of those responsible for the kidnapping of Lorcan's nun, as far as we know.

Still, we hoped to find them alive at least, no matter in what condition.

The radio I just received shattered any illusions about that.

"Our men are already inside the main house. There's nothing there but bodies, Lorcan," I report.

"When did they kill them? Are the bodies already stiff?"

I ask the soldier through the intercom, and shaking my head, I say:

"You'd better see for yourself."

Cillian's brothers, Kellan and Odhran, are with us, as well as Keiron.

The distance between the sand and the headquarters isn't very large, but the building is goddamn strange. It looks more like something medieval with broad stones and high walls, like a fortress.

Or a prison.

The bastard made sure to destroy any chance they had of escaping.

"It seems there isn't a soul here," Keiron says.

That's because there truly isn't. They were slaughtered, according to what our man has just revealed to me.

And then, as we walk, the bodies start to appear.

Young women of all ages, I'd say the youngest around fifteen, up to about twenty-one, wearing nightgowns, the dried blood sticking the clothes to their bodies.

"Jesus Christ!" Keiron says. "They didn't leave any alive."

"It was recent," Kellan, Cillian's brother, says. "No more than twenty-four hours. He knew we were coming."

Almost simultaneously, we think the obvious: it's a trap.

Suddenly, there's a burst of gunfire all at once.

All of this happens in a split second.

I don't have time to think because I see a gun aimed at Lorcan's head.

I step in front and quickly realize that I've been hit in the arm.

The impact, more than the pain, knocks me down, but not before I see the bastard who tried to kill Lorcan fall as well, and around us, it seems like the apocalypse has begun.

The room is dark, and although I'm sure the man who tried to kill me was shot, everyone looks around, guns drawn, unsure if there are more enemies.

Lorcan remains standing, and I touch his ankle to signal him to crouch.

"Fucking suicidal!"

"Fuck! Hang in there!" he shouts when he sees me injured, probably thinking I'm worse off than I actually am.

He crouches, and if I were a sensitive guy, I'd think I'm dying by the look on his face.

"There's no one else!" Kellan shouts. "It was just one," he says, kicking a bastard fallen on the ground.

"Open the windows," Lorcan commands, as Keiron approaches to assess the seriousness of my injury.

"Crazy motherfucker," my friend says only to me. "He'll be fine," he tells the others.

With the light, I see the shooter lying face down on the floor.

"Did you shoot her?" Lorcan asks Kellan.

"Yes. She was aiming at your head. There wasn't time, so she still managed to graze you and also hit Rourke," Kellan replies.

"How could you see her in this goddamn darkness?"

"Despite the sweep our men did, I found it strange that no one had stayed behind," Kellan says.

"And then you saw her? Why didn't you shoot to kill?"

"I'm curious. Why the hell did she want you, specifically?"

He nods and gestures to one of the men to turn the unconscious woman over.

The surprise is that it's not a woman. It's a cross-dressing man.

"What the fuck is this? It's the damned lawyer wearing a dress!" Odhran says, referring to the damn pedophile who owns the island and is a prominent lawyer at one of the most prestigious law firms in the country.

"No, it's his twin," Kellan says, pointing to a message on his watch. "My brother was trying to contact us because Taisiya remembered there were two of them. They're twins."

"Taisiya..." The bastard laughs, spitting blood. "The only one who got away from us."

Hearing him brag about the time they tortured his girl, Lorcan loses it, as if a switch of hatred has been flipped in his body.

He crouches and sticks his finger into the bullet wound, making the bastard scream.

"You're already dead, motherfucker, but it will take you many days to realize it. How could you be so stupid and stay on the island even after you killed them? Even if you had hit me, you would never leave here alive."

I stop paying attention, the numbness spreading through my arm along with a fucking sleepiness.

When I wake up, hours or days later, I have no idea, I realize the bullet has been removed and I'm in a hospital room.

I know it's probably one that only serves Syndicate men. There would be no way to explain to the police the number of injuries our "work" produces every day.

"They knocked you out to bring you on the flight. You were operated on, you crazy bastard," Keiron says.

"How long have I been here?"

"Almost twenty-four hours."

"Tulia..."

"I'll bring her. I knew you'd ask, but I wanted to make sure you were okay before going after the Russian woman," Keiron says.

"I'll survive. It's not the first bullet I've taken, and it won't be the last."

"What was going through your mind?"

Before I can answer, Lorcan enters the clinic room.

"That's what I'd like to know too. I thank you for what you did, but don't risk yourself again, bastard."

I don't know how to handle thanks, so I just stare at him.

"You saved my life, Rourke. I owe you a debt of gratitude. Ask for anything and you shall have it."

I don't hesitate.

"I want Tulia with me."

He first looks at my face as if to laugh, and I think it's because, like everyone else, he knew that Tulia and I had our differences.

"I don't think I understand."

"Tulia is mine."

"She just doesn't know it yet," the mocking bastard Keiron says.

"What do you mean Tulia is *yours*?"

"In the same way that Taisiya belongs to you."

"I'll stay away from Russians from now on," Keiron quips, "there must be some kind of spell on them."

"Tulia is just the daughter of Russians," I snarl.

He shrugs.

"Russian just the same."

"What do you mean you want her, Rourke? Do you have any idea what you're asking me?"

"She's hated within the Organization. She's never had missions beyond deceiving Sierra and babysitting his girl. She's not a key player. She doesn't know anything. She's never killed for them. She was just bait for Leonid's wife, and that sums up all the service she's done for the Russians."

"She's a Russian soldier, damn it. She's received their training. On some level, she's committed."

"A soldier they don't know what to do with. But I do. I want her. She's mine."

I can feel his tension even from a distance, and it's nearly a minute before he speaks again.

"Cillian will go mad. Be sure of what you're asking me, Rourke. She can't be returned if you just get tired of her. It would be a death sentence for the girl."

I hear him, while I remember the last night we spent together.

Her eyes and the plea for it not to end.

"I will never return her."

He turns as if to leave but then stops and turns back.

"And what about you?" he asks Keiron, making it clear that he knows about our past "arrangement."

My friend raises both hands.

"I don't want anyone. If she comes, she'll be a hundred percent Rourke's. I might even be the damn best man at the wedding, but just thinking about sleeping with the same woman for several days in a row gives me a fever."

Lorcan glares at me again.

"If you hurt her, Taisiya will make my life hell, and you can bet your white ass I'll make yours too."

When he leaves, I say to Keiron:

"Go get her for me. I need my blonde with me."

"Don't forget how you parted ways. If you're expecting kisses and cuddles, I'd bet she's going to give you a hard time."

"I don't care. Tulia is worth it."

Chapter 35

Tulia

I couldn't sleep.

An unexplained tightness in my chest, as if someone was sitting on top of it, made me get up and walk around every hour.

After several attempts to get some sleep, I turned to one of my obsessions: organizing anything I could. My OCD is almost uncontrollable.

I've counted and recounted imaginary lines on the wall and also the number of slats in the living room blinds.

Even after tidying up all the kitchen cabinets, the lingerie drawer, changing my nail polish a half dozen times, I still couldn't calm down, so I finally gave up.

I have no doubt that if I keep this up, I'll end up in a mental asylum soon.

The feeling of anguish is so bad that for the first time I thought about taking an anxiety medication my cousin Fanya uses and recommended to me right after I ran away from home.

My mind is playing tricks on me, scaring me, making me check, just to be sure, how they are, if they've returned from that mission — which is crazy, since both are much more experienced soldiers than I'll ever be.

I don't like anything that dulls my senses, but I also don't want to have a heart attack from stress at twenty-three.

The alternative is physical exercise, so I put on my running shoes. I change from jeans to yoga pants and put on a top. I put on my headphones and leave the building with my phone in an armband.

An hour later, I realize I've headed toward Keiron's address — because I have no idea where Rourke lives.

I walk in front of the building like a stalker, but of course, I can't see either of them.

I decide to leave before one of the neighbors calls the police. Or worse, an Irish soldier sees me here and thinks I'm spying on Keiron on Yerik's orders.

That's all I need!

I restart my run, this time at a more moderate pace, and my phone rings.

When I check that it's Taisiya, I stop running to answer her.

"Hi."

"You're out of breath. What happened?"

"I was exercising. I feel jittery. Did something happen?"

"You're not the hysterical type, are you?"

"I wasn't until half a second ago, now my legs feel like jelly. What happened? Rourke, Keiron?"

"Rourke was shot."

"Oh my God!"

"I shouldn't even be telling you this, but I was going to call you anyway because I had an idea about how to get you out of the Organization, at least for a while. Then Lorcan arrived and..."

"Just tell me if he's okay!"

I feel my stomach twist as I remember my Irishman and how I left without saying goodbye, once again running away instead of facing what hurts me.

"It was a gunshot wound to the arm, as far as I know. They removed the bullet."

"I want to see him."

"I was going to call you to come here. Once you're with me, I'll find a way for you to visit him."

"If I go, I'm lost, Taisiya. I've already been forgiven once. I doubt I'll be granted a third chance."

"As I told you, I have a plan, but for that, you need to be safe here with me."

"One thing at a time. I want to see Rourke. If you can make that happen, I'll be forever grateful. I need to touch him and be sure he's okay."

"Have you fallen for him?"

"I don't know if I'm capable of loving again, and I'm not ready to try to interpret feelings at the moment, but I want to be with him."

"Come here. We'll sort it out. I'll talk to Lorcan."

"How's your situation there?"

"I don't know which path we'll take to calm things down, Tulia, but there's nothing to be done. I'm expecting a baby from the man I love, and there isn't a boss in the world who will keep me from being with Lorcan."

I hang up and go back to running. Now, even more distressed than before.

"A gunshot wound to the arm," I tell myself.

It's nothing serious. They told me they've been through much worse situations. I noticed several knife scars on both of their bodies.

"Tulia?" I hear someone call me in surprise as I take off my headphones, just as I'm almost reaching my building's door.

I don't know my neighbors. I'm not the social type, but when I turn around, I see it's Walter, a member of the Organization who, like me, is a second-generation Russian, having been born in the United States as well.

"Hi. What are you doing here?" I ask, without any preamble, and this is my super cute version.

"Direct, huh?"

I feel my face flush.

"I didn't mean to be rude. I'm a bit brusque when I speak."

"No problem. I caught you off guard. And you're right. Better get straight to the point: Yerik wants to see you."

I pray I'm a good actress because right now, I feel like throwing up.

"The Pakhan?" I ask, sounding like an idiot.

"Yep. He asked me to take you to Maxim's house."

"He's in Boston?"

I know Yerik's command center is in Atlanta.

"Yes. He arrived yesterday."

"If you can wait for me to take a shower, I'll meet you downstairs in ten minutes."

"I'm sorry, Tulia, but I was ordered to keep an eye on you."

Now, bile rises at lightning speed to my throat.

"I can't show up to the Pakhan all sweaty."

"I'll wait for you to shower."

"That wasn't a request."

"No, it wasn't. I'll give you a piece of advice because I like you a lot, Tulia: don't make things difficult. The longer you take, the more irritated he will get, and I swear you don't want to see him upset."

"No, of course not. Let's go. I'll get ready quickly."

Besides the fear I feel about this unplanned meeting with the Pakhan, I'm uncomfortable about bringing a stranger into my home. I never receive visitors, but since it's a man I don't know at all, it's even worse.

I walk to the elevator, but he stops me, holding my arm.

"Weren't you exercising? What's two floors compared to a run? Let's take the stairs."

I shrug because he's right.

Usually, that's what I do. I walk up, never missing an opportunity to wear myself out.

We reach my apartment, and I take the key from the side of my sports bra, inserting it into the door.

I turn the handle and open the door, but before I can step inside, I feel all the blood in my body turn to ice.

I turn to face him.

"I didn't say I was running."

He doesn't say anything. He just looks at me in silence.

"And I didn't say I lived on the second floor either."

I try to think quickly about what to do, but before I can take another breath, he covers my mouth and pushes me into the apartment.

Rourke

"YOU'RE A STUBBORN FUCKING mule. The doctor only released you because he was scared, you crazy bastard!" Keiron shouts as we park in front of her building.

I ignore him.

I decided to come meet Tulia myself. The gunshot wound I took wasn't anywhere near the worst in my career. I'll be fine in a week.

We get out of the car and walk to the entrance.

"Do you know the floor?" he asks.

"What do you think? By now I even know her shoe size."

"How can you be sure she's home?"

"I can't, but I'll exhaust all possibilities."

"And what are the other possibilities? You should be resting in your apartment. Or better yet, you shouldn't have left the clinic."

"I can't wait to see her, Keiron. A fucking chain of events has kept me from talking to her. That ends today."

There's no doorman, but just as we arrive, a resident is coming in and, without asking anything, lets us through.

"Great security," I joke.

"You could have used the intercom."

"And risk her not answering me?"

He laughs as we start to climb the stairs.

"Seeing you insecure about a woman is the joke of the century, Rourke. They throw themselves at you, and you never responded. You needed an enemy soldier to make your armor crumble. Do you know the apartment number?" he asks as we reach the second floor.

"No, but I'm ready to ring every doorbell until..."

"Noooooooo!"

The high-pitched scream is unmistakable. It's from a woman, and whoever gave it is terrified.

I feel my pulse quicken and head in the direction I think it came from.

"Noooooo! Let me go!"

"Tulia," both he and I say at the same time.

I don't think, I just act, throwing my body against the door.

Chapter 36

Rourke

It takes three tries before the door finally opens.

And then, I see the nightmare that's haunted me for years unfolding before me. It's like a replay of what happened with Viona.

I see Tulia, her top askew, one side of her face swollen, probably from an assault, and a son of a bitch on top of her.

She struggles to escape, and the bastard is so engrossed in his attack that he doesn't even realize we're no longer alone.

"The knife," I ask Keiron.

I move to where they are and take him from behind in a chokehold. Terrified, he flails, but he'll never be a match for me.

"Who are you?" I ask, leaving just enough space so he doesn't pass out, the knife pressed to his neck.

The wounded arm burns like hell, and I'm almost sure it's started bleeding again, but no army could drag me away from here now.

"He said he came on Yerik's orders," she says, "but I don't believe it. Taisiya would never allow this. She would have warned me or gotten me out of here."

Tulia is in shock, her words coming out in a rush, fear evident in her eyes. Her beautiful face, drenched in tears, is enough to trigger my rage.

"You'll only get one more chance to answer, you son of a bitch."

I tighten my grip. I could kill him with just a twist of my arm, but I need answers first.

"I came on my own. If it hadn't been me, it would have been someone else. The Brotherhood doesn't like our women turning into Irish whores."

He knows he's going to die, so he doesn't bother lying anymore.

"Get her out of here," I tell Keiron. "Take her to the bedroom."

He does as I ask, picking her up in his arms. She allows herself to be cared for without protest, maybe a little out of touch with reality at the moment.

"You and that nun," he starts shouting again, "are nothing but wh..."

I drop the knife and, with one swift movement, snap his neck.

It was quick and almost painless. Far less than he deserved, but we're in her apartment, and I can't draw attention or jeopardize her in any way.

I release the limp body at my feet.

"She's not a whore; she's my wife, you piece of shit."

"GET HER OUT OF HERE," Lorcan says. "Take her to my apartment, and we'll think carefully about what to do next. We need to clean everything up and make sure he was telling the truth and acted alone."

"Regardless, she's not safe anymore. She's staying with me. No, beyond that, I'm not giving her back," I warn.

He looks at me for a few seconds and then nods.

"In your place, I wouldn't give Taisiya back either, but I don't want you staying in the city until we sort this mess out. I have a house in the mountains that no one knows about, in Stowe. It's three hours away. Take her there. I'll send a driver and security with you. We'll sort this out. Be ready in an hour."

Keiron and I head to the bedroom, but before we get there, I ask: "How is she?"

"What do you think? Terrified. There's no way back to the Brotherhood, Rourke. Sooner or later, they'll try again."

"I never intended to allow that, but Tulia can't spend the rest of her life looking over her shoulder. Lorcan needs to talk to Cillian about it."

"He will, I'm sure of it. For now, do what he asked. Get our Russian out of here."

SHE SLEPT THE WHOLE way here.

Keiron and I took her out of the apartment, and when we arrived at my house, a Syndicate doctor was already waiting for us, probably on Lorcan's orders.

He redid my stitches, which had reopened, and examined her.

Aside from the bruise on her face, which I guessed was from a slap that cowardly son of a bitch gave her, she didn't appear to be injured externally. Internally, I'm not so sure.

She allowed herself to be examined like a doll. She didn't speak to any of us, and even when I said we were leaving the city, she didn't protest.

The doctor thought it best to administer a sedative. She passed out still in my room. I carried her to the car, and it's been an hour since we arrived, but she still hasn't woken up.

I chose a suite for the two of us. She may be angry with me if she wants, but I intend to keep watch over her until I'm sure she's awake and not in pain or afraid.

Who am I kidding? I'll keep watch over her even after that.

The curtains in the room are open, and sitting in the armchair, in the dusk of early evening, I can see the mountains of this small Vermont town.

We can't hide here forever, but the idea of being isolated with her, making sure she's safe, is exactly what we need to sort things out.

I don't know what I was dreaming the day Keiron said I called out Viona's name, but it certainly wasn't out of longing as Tulia thought. Long ago, the good dreams with my ex-wife faded, leaving only nightmares.

I don't want them anymore. I lived in the past for years. Tulia is my present and future.

Taisiya

"ANA, YOU NEED TO TALK to Talassa. If anyone can bend the Pakhan, it's her."

We've been on a video call for half an hour, during which I told my sister what happened to Tulia.

I'm still trying to understand how a man from the Brotherhood itself would have the audacity to assault a soldier-member. No matter the excuse the bastard gave himself, Lorcan told me that if the guys hadn't arrived in time, the worst would have happened.

Thinking of Tulia, vulnerable and injured, makes me want to cry. I've grown attached to her in a way I never thought possible. What started with mutual dislike turned into friendship the moment I started to see the hurt girl behind the grumpy soldier.

A bond formed between us, and I will do whatever I can to protect her.

"Taisiya, your situation is already quite precarious. Maxim let slip that there will be a meeting called by Ruslan, between Yerik and Cillian, to decide your and my nephew's father's fate."

"You know perfectly well there's nothing to decide. I'm not leaving him, Anastacia."

"I know, sister. What I'm trying to say is that bringing Tulia's name into the discussion now will only create more tension."

"I will protect her no matter what, Ana."

I hear her sigh on the other end of the line.

"Can we handle one thing at a time, at least? For example, while I haven't talked to Talassa, what will I say if Maxim asks where she is?"

"Tell him she's with me."

"But that's not true, Taisiya."

"Yes, I know, but in that case, I'll be the one lying, not you. I don't want you to be disloyal to your husband because of me."

"It's just a matter of semantics. It doesn't matter where it comes from: I'll be lying anyway."

"Tulia could be dead by now, Ana. If it weren't for Keiron and Rourke's intervention, the outcome would have been different."

"They m..." she starts, but I interrupt her.

"Don't ask me that. It's the kind of thing we don't need to know. If they did, they rid the world of a rapist."

"He was a member of the Brotherhood! How do you think Yerik will react to that?"

"If he's the man Talassa believes he is, he wouldn't allow one of his soldiers to be harmed by a coward."

"Jesus Christ, what a mess!"

"I had an idea, Ana. Talk to Sierra. Tell her what happened. She's the reason Tulia is being punished. If she intervenes on her behalf, it will carry a lot of weight."

"Alright, let's say I convince Sierra to forgive her. And then?"

"One step at a time. Explain to Sierra what Tulia went through and that I want her with me, as a lady-in-waiting. Then, gradually, we'll sort everything out. You're right when you said we should first wait for the meeting between Cillian and Yerik, but I'm sure Ruslan won't let two of his grandsons fight. As for me, things will work out, but that's not enough. I want Tulia protected by my side as well. For now, Sierra is our wild card."

Chapter 37

Tulia

"I dreamed about it."

"Tulia?" he asks. I can sense his surprise at realizing that I'm awake and also the tension in his voice.

I've been awake for about half an hour, but I kept my eyes closed, thinking about what happened.

I was terrified at the time. I fought with everything I could, using all the self-defense techniques I've learned over years of training, and still, it wasn't enough to stop him.

There came a point where I thought I was going to die, but I promised myself that if it happened, I would die fighting.

I had never been physically attacked before. It was frightening, but it's not even close to being as painful as having my heart crushed.

I am a survivor of soul wounds. Now, of body wounds too.

More than ever, I'm certain that I don't want to continue in the Brotherhood.

"Talk to me, baby," he asks, rising and approaching the bed.

He stands a few steps away, and I want to ask him to come closer, to hold me, but I don't have the courage.

I can only see the outline of his body in the semi-darkness, but even having slept for the past few hours, I knew it was Rourke who was here with me.

"What did you dream about, Tulia?"

"You coming after me. Saying that what happened that last night together was real."

"It was real," he says, still not sitting down.

"How could it be, Rourke, if you called out your ex-wife's name in your sleep? Even unconsciously, and while sleeping with another woman, you still missed her?"

He steps back and goes to the window.

Normally, this would be the moment I'd shrink away from an emotional confrontation. I've learned to accept what people are willing to offer me. I never demand "more." But being so close to death may have broken or built—I'm not sure yet—something inside me.

Instead of standing still, waiting for him to take the initiative to speak, I go after him.

I get up and walk to where he is.

He still doesn't turn around.

I move into the space between his body and the window, and now our skins are touching.

He looks at me, and in the moonlight, I can see the pain on his face.

"You still love her."

"I will love her forever, Tulia. There was no way to know Viona and not love her, but I'm sure that wasn't why I called her name that night."

"Did Keiron tell you that was the reason I left?"

"Yes, and I went after you that very day."

"You did?"

He nods.

"I stayed parked outside your apartment, but you had already left."

"I..." I start, completely confused, but before I can say more, he steps away, goes to the lamp, and turns on the light.

"I need to see you while we talk. You'll look into my eyes and judge if I'm telling the truth."

He returns and positions himself in front of me again. Now, however, he has both hands planted on the window behind me, creating a kind of cage.

After what happened earlier today, it would be expected that I would be terrified by the almost confinement his arms create, but I'm not.

The warmth of Rourke and his scent calm me. I feel protected within the fortress of his arms.

"I have recurring nightmares about the day Viona was murdered."

"What?"

I had imagined she had died from a disease, in an accident, or something like that, and now I'm alert to every word.

"We got married because she got pregnant. Viona came to live in Boston as soon as she graduated from High School. Our families had known each other forever. I liked her and I'm monogamous by nature, so even though I wasn't thinking about getting married anytime soon, and without loving her, I did what I thought was right and made her my wife."

I can barely breathe, my head spinning. Nothing he's telling me is like what my insecure heart imagined. I created a fairy tale where his life was perfect until his wife died.

"Please continue."

"I came to love her through living with her. It wasn't an explosive kind of love that makes the blood boil, but the kind of serene love that comes from admiring the person. She was passionate about me, and I loved her. Do you understand the difference?"

"I think so. You were her world. And she was someone who was part of yours."

"Yes. I liked what we had, but I knew that if we ever separated, I would survive. And although the marriage turned out to be better than I initially expected, we fought a lot. I can't say for sure, but I believe that if she were still alive, we might have already divorced."

"Why did you fight?"

"It's hard for someone outside our world to understand the life we lead. When I go on a mission, I can be away for a week. For a couple who has been married for just a few months, I don't think that was ideal."

"You said she was murdered. By some enemy of yours?"

"No." He closes his eyes but doesn't pull away. He remains pressed against me, and I can see how painful it is for him to recall this. "I had gone away on a trip. She was quite far along in her pregnancy. Even though I had men watching over her when I was away, as soon as I arrived, I would go get her wherever she was. That day, Viona had gone to a party."

"From the Syndicate? I mean, with women from the Syndicate?"

"No. She had friends from the store where she worked. It was a bachelorette party, if I'm not mistaken. Anyway, when I arrived to pick her up, she was drunk. It pissed me off a lot."

"Because of the pregnancy?"

"Yes. I was excited about the idea of becoming a father, so in my spare time, I studied everything I could about babies and the healthy development of the fetus. According to some experts, women who drink regularly while pregnant risk having a child with what is called fetal alcohol syndrome, and it was already the fourth time Viona had drunk excessively within a span of thirty days. Children born with this syndrome can suffer from physical and mental disorders."

"Oh my God, I had no idea."

"Yes, so you can imagine that I wasn't thrilled to see my wife, who was due to give birth in a couple of months, completely drunk to the point of not being able to stand up."

"Jesus!"

"We went home. She said a lot of bullshit on the way. I ignored it. I'm not the type to argue because when I say something, I don't apologize later; it's intentional. So, I let her vent. It wouldn't be the first or last fight we'd have, I thought."

"But it was the last one, wasn't it?"

"Yes. We got home, and I helped her take a shower. I tried to give her something to eat. She refused. I was reaching my limit, so I went to sleep. She wanted to stay in the living room. In the middle of the night, I heard the door slam. I was sleepy and still angry. I didn't get up."

I hold my breath, feeling that the moment when everything changed in his life is approaching.

"What happened?"

"She left the house, in her nightgown. I'll never understand why she did that. I think she was still drunk or maybe very angry. We both had fiery tempers. I woke up hours later. Viona still hadn't returned and it was cold outside. I started to worry when I walked around our neighborhood and couldn't find her. So, I called Keiron and we organized a search with the Syndicate's men."

I'm trembling. I can feel his pain in every cell of my body and I want to make it go away, but I know from my own experience that it's impossible.

"We found her body late in the afternoon." He takes a step back. "She had been raped and killed by a serial killer. It was a random crime. Viona was in the wrong place at the wrong time. He was prowling, looking for a victim, and saw her, alone and vulnerable."

I don't care if he wants me near him right now. I go to him and grab him around the waist, pulling him close.

"Did you catch him?"

"Yes. I hunted him down and killed him."

"I hope he suffered."

"He did suffer, but it would never be enough to make up for the lives he destroyed."

"You blame yourself."

"How could I not blame myself, Tulia? I should have taken better care of her."

"You did what you could, Rourke. If there's one thing I've learned, it's that we have to deal with the consequences of our actions. What happened was a tragedy. It wasn't anyone's fault. Neither yours nor Viona's. It was just a matter of chance that she crossed paths with that monster."

He wraps his arms around me, and for many minutes, I let myself stay like this, without saying a word.

"When I saw you hurt today, it was like revisiting a nightmare. Again, my vulnerable wife in the hands of a son of a bitch."

I feel my heart pounding in my ear.

"Your *wife*?"

"You are mine, Tulia. I knew that the moment I saw you. I don't like comparing, but I can't find another way to explain what you mean to my life. I told you that Viona was a kind of *learned* love. I loved her through living with her and the circumstances because she was an amazing person. I didn't resist the feeling. With you, it was different. The moment I met you, even back at that bar, I wanted to make you mine. I knew you were mine."

"You seemed to hate me."

"Part of me might have hated you, but not for the reason you think. I didn't want anyone in my life. I had already resigned myself to punishing myself forever, living in a sea of guilt. Then you came along and I couldn't get you out of my head."

"Physical attraction."

"At first, yes. But every time I saw you, when you came with Taisiya, it felt like walking toward the inevitable. With or without a snowstorm, there would come a time when I couldn't keep denying the desire to be with you."

I rest my forehead against his chest, trying to control what these words are doing to me, but it's no use.

I'm tired of protecting myself from the pain. I want to take the leap into the void, and I want it to be with him.

"I was on my way to meet Taisiya when Walter attacked me. She told me she'd find a way for me to see you. I was terrified when I learned you had been shot."

I look at him again and notice that his face has cleared.

"If I had known that dying was the only way to make you fall in love with me, I would have arranged a shootout earlier."

"Don't joke about that. Besides, I didn't say anything about love and..."

I don't finish the sentence because he holds my face and kisses me.

At first, I think it's to silence me, but then, the longing and then the desire explode between us as they did the first time we touched.

He picks me up and carries me to the bed.

In seconds, we're naked, but he slows his movements, hovering over my body, nestled between my legs.

"I'm crazy about you, Tulia. I didn't even see you coming. You messed up my plans to stay alone. You are the uncertainty and the risk. We have everything to go wrong, but I won't let it happen. You're my prisoner, Russian. You're never leaving."

He doesn't wait for a response after the "threat." He enters me, taking me completely.

My body responds to his, liquid fire coursing through my veins.

Rourke looks at me every time he thrusts into me, and at that moment, I feel desired, but also protected and cherished.

When he lowers his head and licks one breast and then the other, I become dizzy with pleasure.

I pull his face and press our lips together. My tongue inviting him to possess me, saying, without words, that I'm letting all my barriers fall for him, for both of us.

He seems to understand my surrender, because the way he takes me now is not just erotic; it's intimate too.

Rourke possesses me as if he wants to mark me, to erase any doubt that we belong to each other.

He swivels his hips and I scream, uncontrollably, because he seems to know how to reach all the right places inside me.

I feel him throbbing, thickening and tightening inside me.

He says dirty words, and his filthy mouth drives me even crazier.

I bite his neck and chest, unable to stay still.

I want to lick him all over.

"I need it harder," he says. "Are you in any pain?"

"No. Do it," I beg.

He rides me, looking into my eyes, and his hand slides to my clitoris, stimulating it.

He increases the rhythm and I'm on the edge of the precipice that will lead me to orgasm.

"Rourke..."

The thrusts increase and when he grabs my ass, lifting me off the bed, I come.

He still thrusts a few more times inside me and then, I feel his warmth filling me after he plunges in one last time.

I CONTINUE HOLDING him between my thighs, my legs locked around his waist, and then, suddenly, I remember:

"Oh my God, Rourke. Your arm!"

"It's fine. The doctor redid the stitches," he says, kissing my forehead. Then his face becomes serious. "We need to talk about what's going to happen from now on. About our future."

"I'm not going to discuss anything with you while you're still inside me. I'm at a disadvantage."

"From where I'm sitting, the disadvantage is mine, baby. I can't think straight being caught in the heat of your pussy."

"Then let me go."

"No. Not now, not from the bed, and not from my life. Consider yourself kidnapped, Tulia. I'm not letting you go back to the Organization."

Finally, he slowly withdraws from my body, turns us around, and lays me on top of him.

"I want you to come live with me."

"Live with you?"

"Move in with me."

"You must be crazy! Yerik, Cillian, or both will kill us."

I try to get up, but he won't let me.

"They won't. Lorcan is already working on it."

"Lorcan also has his neck on the line right now."

"No. There will be a meeting among the Syndicate heads. They'll have to come to an agreement about Taisiya, and that includes you."

I look at him, angry.

"I'm not merchandise."

"No, you're my *property*."

He's mocking, but it still annoys me.

"You're a caveman."

"Yes, I am. Now that's established, I'm telling you that I'm not going to let you go back to your apartment again. We're going to try, blonde. It's not a request; it's a warning."

"We're infatuated. This isn't love, Rourke."

"We don't know each other enough to love yet, but I'm crazy about you."

"I don't dislike you either," I admit and receive a slap on the ass. "Alright, let's say I'm a little crazy about you too."

"Improve that speech, woman."

I hold his face and look at him seriously.

"I'm crazy about you too, Irishman. But even if we weren't from rival organizations, I don't see how we could work. We're broken, Rourke."

"Let me piece you back together then. I don't care if, in the end, the result isn't perfect. I want you anyway."

"I'm terrified. If something happens to you because of me..."

He places two fingers over my lips.

"We live in a risky world. A much more dangerous one than that of regular people. Nothing is guaranteed, Tulia, but still, you're worth it and I'm not giving up on that. You're welcome to try to convince me otherwise, try to tell me that you're not mine, but I'm already warning you that you'll never succeed. I said I was broken. I thought I didn't have a heartbeat in my chest anymore. I was wrong. I do. And it's yours."

Days Later

"I FORGIVE YOU, TULIA."

"Sierra?"

"How many enemies do you have besides me?"

I had been keeping the phone off, following Rourke's advice to avoid being located, but this morning, Taisiya sent a message saying Sierra would call me.

"Just you," I reply seriously. "Or maybe now all the men in the Organization as well."

She sighs.

"I'm sorry for what happened."

I'm not surprised she already knows. Taisiya told me, in a phone call the day after I arrived here, that she asked Ana to talk to the wives of Pakhan's trusted men, especially Talassa and Sierra, about my situation.

My future ex-nun friend said all my chances were in the hands of those women. Only they could reverse the situation.

So, when she informed me that Sierra wanted to speak with me, my hopes were renewed.

"It wasn't your fault."

"In a way, it was. My anger towards you made everyone in the Brotherhood hate you too."

"No, Sierra. That bastard attacked me because he found out I was involved with an Irishman."

"And why the hell did you do that?"

"I could return the question by asking how you ended up pregnant by a mortal enemy of your father."

"For someone with a sword hanging over her head, you're quite cheeky. Before we start fighting again, I want you to know that I've forgiven you and not only that: we, the wives of the leaders, have come together to convince our husbands that you should be able to stay with Taisiya."

"I'm not staying with her."

"Listen to me, Tulia. I know you love him, but at first, you need to be discreet. I believe that over time, we can organize your definitive exit from the Brotherhood, but for now, let's allow our men to live under the illusion that they're still in control. Can you do that?"

"I'm in love, Sierra."

"I got that part. It would be the only reason for someone to risk their neck this way."

"No, regardless of Rourke, I was already thinking of leaving. I don't want to live my life deceiving someone like I did with you. Hurting anyone, physically or emotionally. Your forgiveness means a lot to me."

"I'm resentful, Tulia. I hold grudges, but I realized it's a kind of poison. I won't promise that we'll be best friends, but I can swear I'll do whatever I can to defend your position within the Brotherhood."

Chapter 38

Rourke

Boston

One Month Later

"**T**his was the last time you'll sleep here," I tell her as I walk into one of the apartments in Lorcan's building.

The entire building belongs to Cillian, which has allowed us the freedom to sleep together every night since we returned from Vermont. Still, it's not what I want. Tulia belongs in my home and bed.

"What does that mean?"

"From our side, you were already protected from the moment I told Lorcan we were together, but now he's managed to convince Ruslan to intercede on our behalf. You're mine for good, Russian."

"You sound like a caveman." She feigns annoyance.

"And you love it," I say, stealing a kiss from her.

"I do, but I don't like to admit it."

"Let's go home, baby. It's time to start living our story."

"I thought that's what we were doing."

"You still weren't sure about how I feel."

She blushes, and I can tell I've hit the mark.

"And now, do I?"

"Yes, you finally understand that I'm in love and that it's not going away."

"Nothing in life is guaranteed."

"My love for you is, Tulia. It happened so fast that I didn't even have time to turn my back."

"And would you have turned your back?"

"I didn't think I deserved a second chance. But you know what I realized?"

She shakes her head.

"It's not a second chance; it's the first. I've never felt this way before. You're my only one."

"Don't say that if it's not how you truly feel, Rourke. I've had my heart broken before. I don't need promises."

"But I'll make them, baby. Day after day, until you understand that we're both a *forever*.

Tulia

Two Months Later

I HAVEN'T BEEN HERE in a long time.

I no longer need to run from myself like before. I like my life.

I love who I've become, even before I met Rourke.

Today, however, I have a mission.

"Are you sure you want to do this, beautiful?" Keiron asks by my side, before we get out of the car at the cemetery entrance.

"I need to. I'm not jealous of her, Keiron. What happened to Viona and the baby was a tragedy, but I don't blame myself for being happy with the man who was her love."

"Then why come?"

"I want to talk to her. I don't plan on becoming a frequent visitor. My time for visiting graves has passed."

"I don't need to tell you that this obsession of yours was really fucking weird, right?"

I smile, remembering the day I told him that. His face was priceless, like he was dealing with a dangerous lunatic.

"I liked the solitude and peace of the place."

"God forbid!"

"For a ruthless mobster, you're really quite timid."

"No, I just respect the dead. And I'll never understand why you want to visit Viona's grave."

"Thanks for coming with me. I don't know how Rourke would interpret such a request and since you still don't let me go alone..."

"It's for your own safety, Tulia. Yerik gave Cillian his word that nothing would happen to you two, and I believe he'll keep it, especially now that they've formed an alliance against the Sicilians, but Rourke still wants to find out who the other men were who were angry with you inside the Brotherhood, besides that asshole who attacked you."

I close my eyes and can relive the scene as if it were today.

I shiver, and he notices, pulling me into a hug.

"You're ours, blonde. We'll never let anyone hurt you."

He gives me a kiss on the cheek and gets out of the car to open my door.

We walk in silence toward the headstone, but when Keiron guides me to the opposite side from where I was going, I freeze in place.

It's like time rewound to the last day I was here.

"What's wrong?" he asks, probably wondering why I stopped walking.

"It was him," I say, pointing to Rourke, who is about a hundred meters from us, in front of a headstone.

"What?"

"The last time I was here, I saw a man—him, now I know—right there, looking thoughtful."

He follows my gaze to where I'm pointing but seems to misinterpret what I'm saying.

"Don't be upset, love. He always comes."

"That's not it. I'm not angry, but don't you see, Keiron? It was our destiny to meet. I almost passed him that day I'm telling you about, but then I decided to change my path so that the man—Rourke—could grieve in peace."

"I never doubted that, Tulia. You were always meant to be together. Do you want me to go over there with you?"

"No, I'll do this alone. Thank you for bringing me."

He kisses my hand and steps back. As I start walking again, I realize Rourke was watching us.

His face shows a confused and anxious expression, certainly thinking I followed him.

"I'm not angry," I say at the same time he says:

"I came to say goodbye."

I go to where he is and hug him.

"I came to meet her."

Only then do I notice that near the larger headstone there is a small grave—their baby's grave, which, when Viona was killed, was already fully formed.

God!

"You speak first," I request.

"I came to tell her about you and say that she will always have a special place in my heart, but that I've moved on."

"If Viona was the incredible person you told me about, I'm sure she'll be happy for you, Rourke."

"Yes."

"You never talk about the baby."

"I can't yet. I can only handle one thing at a time, Tulia."

"No one's in a hurry here, Irish."

One Year Later

I GLANCE SURREPTITIOUSLY at him, who has an expression as if he's being tortured.

"You hate these movies."

I'm fascinated by romantic comedies, and he's into action films.

We're the most cliché couple on the face of the Earth: girls on one side, playing with dolls, boys on the other, with their toy cars.

"I hate them with every cell in my body, but I love you, and it's worth going through this suffering."

I was smiling, but after what he says, I freeze.

"What did you say?"

Even though I'm now sure we love each other madly, we've never put it into words.

He doesn't answer, gets up, and grabs the popcorn bucket we had left on the coffee table.

We ate only half of it.

"Come here," he says, extending his hand to me, and I look at him confused. But as soon as I stand up, he drops to one knee, still holding the popcorn, and my heart goes wild in my chest.

He reaches into the bucket and pulls out a small, unmistakable box.

"I love you, my Russian. We started out hating each other or pretending to hate each other, but the truth is, ever since I saw you bent over the pool table holding that cue... — He pauses. — All I could think about was how nice it would be to have your hand around my cock."

I was almost crying, but I start to laugh, and I think that was his intention. Rourke isn't one for jokes.

"I don't know if I deserve you, but I'll do everything to prove that I do. Marry me, Tulia."

I nod, signaling yes, and offer my hand for him to place the beautiful ring with a heart-shaped diamond on it.

"No words?"

"I'm not good with them, Rourke, but there's one thing I know how to do right: love you, my Irish."

Epilogue 1

Keiron

"Are you sure about this?" Rourke asks as if he's trying to look inside me.

"Don't dig too deep. There's nothing in here," I joke, tapping my chest over my heart.

He doesn't smile back, but what's new? My best friend is the most moody bastard in the world.

"I feel like I'm stealing her. Don't get me wrong. Tulia is mine. I'd take her from any bastard without a second thought, but we're talking about you."

"If I told you I wanted to be with her *too*, would you share her? Or better yet, if I told you I've discovered that the Russian is the love of my life, would you give up your woman?"

"No. The only way I'd walk away would be if she asked me to," he says. "Now answer this: if I didn't exist, would you settle down with Tulia? Would you make her your wife?"

"I don't have a precise answer for you at the moment."

"From where I'm standing, it's a simple matter."

"It's not. I felt connected to her like I've never felt with anyone else. Tulia is beautiful and sexy. Although she constantly tries to prove she's a *bad girl*, she's as sweet as honey. She's also one of us, she understands the kind of life we lead and that tomorrow isn't a certainty, which makes her the perfect partner. The problem is that I'm not looking for a *forever*.

"Do you plan to stay alone for the rest of your damn life on this planet?"

"I'm never alone," I joke. "Besides, I didn't say anything about loneliness. I have more women in my phone book than I can handle. If in the future that doesn't satisfy me, I might try to find someone who accepts that I'll never be faithful."

"An open relationship?"

I shrug.

"Who cares about the label? The fact is, I know myself. I don't think I'm capable of staying with the same woman for an entire lifetime. My nature isn't to be tied down in an exclusive relationship. I like the beginnings. The thrill of the chase."

He shakes his head, smiling.

"We're all like that until we find the one who makes us want to stay."

"The first time you settled down, it wasn't love at first sight. You learned to love Viona, but you married her because she was pregnant."

"Yes, it wasn't love. It was a sense of responsibility that turned into love with our time together. I was too young and grew up being taught that family and duty go hand in hand. Looking back, it was a mistake. Even though we fell in love over the course of the marriage, there wasn't a real connection. She tried to change me to fit what she needed, and I don't think we'd still be together if not for..."

He stops speaking, and I know this is something he'll never be able to think about without pain, just as it is for me regarding my sister.

Guilt is a damn poison. We take a dose with every memory.

"And what is it about Tulia that makes you want to settle down again?"

"Love. The craziest kind. The kind that's worth it. There's a lot of war between us. Small daily battles over everything and anything, but there's also the eye contact. The search in the middle of the night. Being able to hold her in my arms after fucking her all night long is the highlight of my day."

"You're a prince," I tease. "You manage to combine sleaze and romance in the same statement. If you're so sure you want her, why did you come ask me if I'd be with her if you didn't exist?"

"To see if I'd need to kill you," he says, but he isn't smiling.

I don't think Rourke would actually go so far as to threaten my life, but it's clear he regrets having shared her.

"So it's a good thing I'm leaving."

"Is it because of us?"

"No, although I can't deny that I wouldn't be able to kill the desire I feel for her all of a sudden. Let's say it's because of the three of us. For me, because I want to continue my life as a gigolo," I say, trying to lighten the mood, but again he doesn't smile. "I'm not in love with her, Rourke. What happened was something that will stay in my memory as a great moment, but it was clear, even on those days we spent trapped in the snowstorm, that the connection between you two was total. And, mostly, real on a level I never wanted for myself. I still don't. However, if one day I change my mind about a threesome..."

I say that more to provoke him than because I think it would actually work. I had my first threesome with them, and at the time, there were no feelings involved on either side. If I were to be with Tulia now, even with her and Rourke's consent, I would feel like I was betraying my friend.

"You're like a brother, Keiron. We've almost died together multiple times and you've been by my side at the worst moment of my life, but what happened won't happen again. She needed to free herself from the past; now she needs to have the dreams that were stolen from her come true."

"And *you*, what do you need?"

"To breathe her in for as long as there's air in my lungs. I'm crazy about her."

Dublin — Ireland

Two Months Later

"WHY CAN'T IT BE JUST mine, Keiron?" the hot redhead sitting on my right thigh asks.

"I'm not into possessive pronouns, baby. I'm all yours when we're together, but tomorrow, I don't know if I'll still be interested."

"You're such a bastard."

"I can't deny it, baby. Now, lose that frown. Aggressiveness doesn't suit your beauty. Am I making you miss anything? Once a week, you have me in the palm of your hand."

"And it's always worth it," she says, smiling. "I'm going to dance and I'll be right back."

She stands up and joins her friends, all of whom are my girlfriends on different days of the week. I think I've finally found the perfect arrangement. The best of both worlds: a harem.

I don't get bored, they don't get bored, everyone is happy.

How long this will satisfy me, I have no idea, but I'm still young. Marriage or even settling down with just one partner doesn't cross my mind.

For twenty-four hours, I can be faithful. That's my limit. I almost feel like a serious guy now. Aside from the seven regulars, I don't fuck anyone else.

Occasionally, I think about Tulia, but I force myself to stop.

I could never be what she needs.

Rourke is the complement. I was just a passing storm.

"Come dance, Keiron!" my women shout, laughing.

Maybe the time will come when they realize I'm a bad bet.

They all try to change me. None have succeeded so far.

Eventually, they give up.

And when that happens, I start all over again.

Epilogue 2

Tulia

Tulia and Rourke's Wedding Day

I touch up my lipstick and smooth out my white, tight, strapless knee-length dress, my heart racing for what's about to happen.

Our wedding will be a small, intimate ceremony for a few guests.

The only women present will be Mrs. Orla, the boss's aunt, and Lorcan, Juno, and Taisiya.

Even Fanya didn't want to come. Although I assured her that I would be safe among the Irish for the duration of our celebration, she still said in her characteristic blunt manner, "No, thank you, be happy."

I didn't mind.

For someone who has been alone for so many years, the people gathered here are the equivalent of a crowd.

I hear a knock at the door and say they can come in, but when I see who it is, I run into the arms of my visitor.

"You came!"

"I wouldn't miss it for the world, Russian. You and that bastard of your fiancé are among my two favorite people in the world."

"Does this mean you'll be going back to Boston?"

"Yes. I even met a new girlfriend yesterday."

"Jesus, Keiron, you don't waste any time. You'll never settle down."

"Maybe I will if I ever meet someone like you."

"You never wanted anything serious."

"You were his from the first glance, Tulia, so I took what I could."

"I was his from the first glance," I confirm.

"Besides, I couldn't promise to stay faithful. Even if it were different, if your heart didn't belong to my best friend, eventually, if we were together, I would end up hurting you."

"Do you know one of the things I love most about you?"

"There are so many?"

"Don't be conceited."

"Speak."

"Your honesty, Keiron. Given how I was deceived, sincerity in my world is worth its weight in gold. I respect you for never deceiving the women you get involved with."

"Yes, I know. I'm a prince."

"I didn't say that. You're a decadent bastard, but also one of the best human beings I've ever met."

Rourke told me that as soon as Viona died, Keiron moved into his house, not allowing him to drown in guilt.

The friendship between them is beautiful to see.

"I was afraid you wouldn't come. I didn't understand your departure to Ireland. Did it have to do with us?"

"No. I mean, what happened between us was my first threesome and since Rourke fell in love with you and is my best friend, I thought the three of us needed some time apart."

I don't know how to respond to that. What happened in the snowstorm was very exciting, but today it only represents a memory for me.

I still find Keiron attractive, but now I see him as I would a brother. My heart only has room for one man, and that's Rourke.

My broken, passionate, and loyal Irishman.

The one who holds me in his arms every night, whether we're making love or fucking.

The one I want to spend the rest of my life with.

"Hey, don't think about it. I had a lot of fun in Ireland."

"I know you did, shameless. A girlfriend for each day of the week. Rourke told me."

"You snitching bastard."

"We have no secrets. Keep that in mind when you think about telling him that you passed out after fucking five times in a row," I tease, remembering one of his sexual feats reported by my fiancé.

"The woman was insatiable."

I shake my head, laughing, and then hold his face. Standing on tiptoe, I give him a kiss on the cheek.

"I love you, Keiron. Be happy the way you are. Screw the 'happily ever after' rules."

"You welcomed them."

"Because I found the one who will be my only. We're not perfect, but we're perfect together."

AS I WALK DOWN THE small aisle that Mrs. Orla set up in her garden, arm in arm with Keiron, I can't take my eyes off Rourke.

I had to run away, break and piece myself back together.

I had to lose people and myself, do a complete turnaround in life to finally find the one who has become the absolute master of my heart.

Rourke comes to meet us and after giving me a kiss on the forehead, Keiron hands me over to his best friend.

"Take care of her, bastard," he says.

"Don't doubt it, brother."

After Keiron steps back, my fiancé whispers:

"Ready to become mine?"

"Ready to sign a mere dotted line, Irishman. I've always been yours."

Epilogue 3

Rourke

Three Years Later

"Jesus, two girls in three years?" Keiron says, smiling, as we leave my eldest daughter's room, Colleen. "Do you plan to repopulate the planet on your own? And next time, please, have a boy. We need more men on the team to help fend off the bastards who'll be all over them."

"Buddy, with the mother they have, we don't need any help sending the suitors running. A look from Tulia can make a guy piss his pants. Believe me, she's much scarier when she wants to be than the two of us combined."

My wife is nursing our youngest, Mckenna, and should join us for dinner any moment now.

I was surprised when she told me that Keiron would be coming, given that Fridays are his days for debauchery.

"And the twins?" I ask.

I know that during his time in Ireland, he had a sort of harem where he dated a girl each day, remaining faithful to all, according to his own words. Since then, it seems he's taken a liking to managing semi-fixed relationships simultaneously.

"It didn't work out."

"You seemed really excited when you talked about them the week before last."

"It was just initial excitement. I tried to do the same as in Ireland, seeing one and then the other on alternate days, spreading love equally."

"Certainly easier than being with seven at the same time."

"Yes, that was a wild time in my life."

"Keiron, I'm going to enjoy watching you get so screwed over by a woman one day... I'll sit, drink my beer, and enjoy the show. I know when it hits, it's going to be tough."

"Don't jinx me. It's never going to happen. Proof of that is I couldn't keep up with the twins. They were identical, so alternating days between them didn't help; it always felt like I was with the same woman. I got bored very quickly."

I can't help but laugh.

"Jesus Christ, keep it down, I just got the baby to sleep," Tulia says, entering the room with a murderous expression.

"I couldn't help it, baby."

"Boy's secret?"

"No," he replies and explains to her the reason for my laughter.

Tulia laughs too.

"One day, you'll meet a woman who will bring you to your knees, my friend," she prophesies.

"No chance. I'll never be faithful," he says arrogantly.

I NOTICE WHEN SHE OPENS the bedroom door and watches as I lay our youngest in the crib.

It's a ritual I perform every night. I always make time for our girls. As much as possible, I manage my time to tell the stories they love before they fall asleep.

The eldest understands now; Mckenna doesn't, but I don't mind. I want them to know that I'll always be around for them and because of them.

Some psychologists might say it's a way of redeeming the loss of my first child. I don't care for explanations; I do what my instinct and heart tell me.

Just before my first daughter was born, I finally managed to talk to someone — to Tulia — for the first time about how I felt about the death of my son, the child I only knew in a coffin.

When Viona was pregnant, I wanted the baby, but it was only later that I realized how much I already loved him. It took the tragedy for me to understand that after he was gone, a piece of my heart died with him.

I push the thought away because I don't want Tulia to realize that, occasionally, I still enter my dark rooms.

When I reach the door, she has both hands on her belly, where our third child, now a boy, is being carried.

In just over four months, Rí will be with us.

"You are the best father in the world," she says, as if sensing that I was thinking of our deceased son.

"I try to be. And as a husband? What do you say?"

"The best I ever dreamed of, my Irishman."

The End!

Did you love *Forbidden Desires*? Then you should read *Indecent Protection* by Amara Holt!

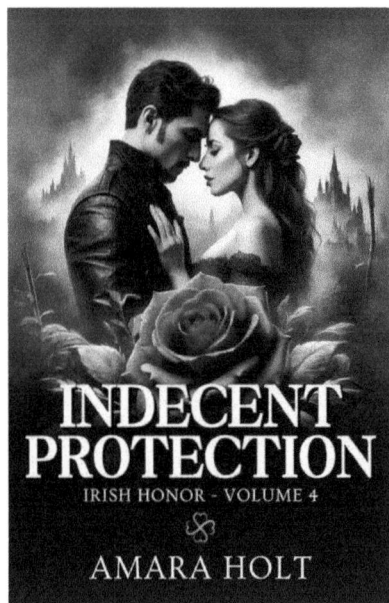

Indecent Protection

Elaine has always kept her life under tight control, but when a **ruthless past** comes back to haunt her, threatening the safety of her beloved nephew, she has no choice but to turn to the one man she's feared the most—Odhran. Known as the "**Mad Lion**" of the Irish Syndicate, Odhran is notorious for his **explosive temper** and his unyielding demand for loyalty. He's the kind of man you never want as an enemy—but for Elaine, he might be her only hope.

Odhran desires Elaine with a **burning intensity** that goes beyond reason. He doesn't do long-term relationships, but he's determined to keep her by his side, no matter the cost. In exchange for his protection, she must **surrender herself** to him, becoming his in a way she never imagined possible. The deal is dangerous, the attraction undeniable, and the consequences could be deadly.

As danger closes in from all sides, Elaine finds herself trapped in a **perilous dance** with the devil himself. Will she survive the twisted game of power and passion, or will she lose everything—including her heart—to the **Mad Lion**?

Indecent Protection is a dark, suspenseful romance that will keep you on the edge of your seat. Perfect for fans of mafia romances, this book delves into the gritty underworld of **power, control,** and the dangerous allure of **forbidden love.**

About the Author

Amara Holt is a storyteller whose novels immerse readers in a whirlwind of suspense, action, romance and adventure. With a keen eye for detail and a talent for crafting intricate plots, Amara captivates her audience with every twist and turn. Her compelling characters and atmospheric settings transport readers to thrilling worlds where danger lurks around every corner.

Milton Keynes UK
Ingram Content Group UK Ltd.
UKHW030146051224
452010UK00001B/108

9 798330 596386